Jury Pool

A Killer's Mind

Sissy Marlyn

Copyediting by Robert Ritchie

BEARHEAD PUBLISHING

- BhP -

Louisville, Kentucky

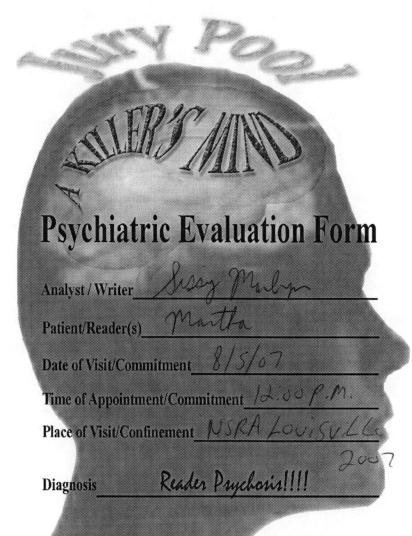

Psychiatric Evaluation Form

Analyst / Writer _Sissy Marilyn_

Patient/Reader(s) _Martha_

Date of Visit/Commitment _8/5/07_

Time of Appointment/Commitment _12:00 P.M._

Place of Visit/Confinement _NSRA Louisville 2007_

Diagnosis _Reader Psychosis!!!!_

Martha,
Enjoy!
Sissy

BEARHEAD PUBLISHING

- BhP -

Louisville, Kentucky
www.sissymarlyn.com

A Killer's Mind
by Sissy Marlyn
Copyediting by Robert Ritchie

Copyright © 2007 Mary C. Drechsel
ALL RIGHTS RESERVED

Cover Design by Bearhead Publishing
First Printing - March 2007
ISBN: 0-9776260-8-3

Disclaimer

This book is a work of fiction. The characters, names, places, and incidents are used fictitiously and are a product of the author's imagination. Any resemblance of actual persons, living or dead is entirely coincidental.

NO PART OF THIS BOOK MAY BE REPRODUCED
IN ANY FORM, BY PHOTOCOPYING OR BY ANY
ELECTRONIC OR MECHANICAL MEANS,
INCLUDING INFORMATION STORAGE OR
RETRIEVAL SYSTEMS, WITHOUT PERMISSION
IN WRITING FROM THE COPYRIGHT OWNER/AUTHOR

Proudly Printed in the United States of America.

Acknowledgements

Thanks to the following great people, places, or things that helped to add flavor, description, and life to *A Killer's Mind*:

Old Hickory Lake – Hendersonville, TN

Hendersonville Police Department – Hendersonville, TN

Gaylord Entertainment Center – Nashville, TN

Metropolitan Nashville Police Department, Criminal Investigation Division, Homicide Section Nashville, TN
Lt. Patrick J. Taylor
CIO/Homicide - Cold Case

Commander Andy Garrett
Central Patrol Precinct

The Eagles – what an awesome, timeless band

Greenview Medical Center
Bowling Green, KY

Nashville Railroad Bridge
Historical and still going strong.

Marvel Comics – For creating *The Incredible Hulk*

Other Novels Written by *Sissy Marlyn*:

Intimacies
Illusions
Indecisions
(A trilogy of Women's Fiction Novels)

Jury Pool
(The predecessor to this novel)

Bardstown
(The beginning of another Women's Fiction trilogy)

For more information and synopsis of each novel, check
www.sissymarlyn.com

Dedication

To all law enforcement officials:
We wouldn't be safe without you!

To the psychiatric community:
You tirelessly try to heal troubled human minds.

To Bearhead and Nalla Cat:
For their continued support.
I love you guys bunches!

Prologue

Old Hickory Lake rippled with the light morning breeze. A hovering mist slowly dissipated with the appearance of the rising sun. Sun rays, images of billowing clouds, looming trees, underbrush, and the silhouette of a red-haired man, standing on a dock, danced in the slow moving stream.

With care and expertise, Jack Jordan cast a line from his fishing rod. The whiz disturbed the joyful chirping of birds in the trees. Jack's floater landed, with a soft splash, far into the lake, forming circles all about its site. With the return of silence, the birds resumed their melodic serenade.

A bucket beside Jack already held a bass he had caught that morning. He had caught several smaller fish as well, but he had thrown them back into the lake.

Since retiring from a thirty year deputy sheriff position in Louisville, Kentucky and buying a small house in Hendersonville, Tennessee, Jack routinely visited one of the fishing docks at nearby Old Hickory Lake a few mornings a week. He enjoyed the peace and solitude of fishing at dawn. He also enjoyed the fish dinners he prepared for himself.

Jack's ear caught a creak in one of the boards on the dock behind him. Partially turning his head, out of the corner of his eye, Jack spied a curious raccoon studying him. Disinterested in the escapades of this pesky animal, Jack focused his attention back to the lake and his bobber.

A downward movement of his floater and a tug on his fishing line engrossed Jack's focus. The boards in back of him creaked some more and the dock moved, but Jack paid no heed to this distraction. Instead, he fully concentrated on setting his fishing line, intent on catching another fish.

A moment later, Jack's rod and reel bounced off the end of the dock with a clatter and landed with a splash in the water. The fish on the other end of the line erratically zigzagged the loose reel across the lake. The dock clunked, rocking like a ship tossed by waves. Tree branches popped and swung; bushes fanned. Birds darted in all directions. Their flapping wings and chimes of distress turned the once peaceful atmosphere into pandemonium. The pesky raccoon tore a new path through the forest.

Jack lay on his back on the swaying dock. A fountain of red gushed from a cavernous wound across his neck, spilling down and re-coloring the gray planks around him. Flowing between openings in the boards, his blood resonated a consistent 'drip, drip, drip' in the water below. Jack's body thrashed about and gurgling noises erupted as he struggled to draw his final breath. Large, glassy, horror-filled, baby-blue eyes starred up at his attacker.

With a satisfied smirk on his face, Jack's executioner raised his knife again, plunging it downward, leaving his final mark – *my calling card*. Jackson Charles Jordan ceased to be.

Chapter 1

The Break

Scott Arnold's arm whipped out and knocked over an empty can of coke from his bedside table. The clatter from the can bouncing across the hardwood floor completely aroused him from his sleep. His hand, at last, managed to snatch a bellowing telephone. Pushing the button and turning the phone on, he pulled it to his ear and muttered, "Hello."

"Sleeping, Rookie?" a familiar voice he had not heard in awhile asked.

Scott slid to a sitting position in the bed. He glanced at a bedside clock and struggled to focus. A bright red **6:30** swam before his eyes. If Roger Matthews was calling him, especially at this early hour, what he had to say must be important. Roger was Scott's ex-partner from the Louisville Homicide Squad.

"What's up, Roger?" Scott asked, running a hand over his face and stretching to erase the last remnants of sleep.

"*You...now*," Roger kidded with a chuckle.

"Come on, Roger. I know you didn't call this early to mess with me," Scott said, impatient and a little irritated. He had been up past midnight getting the goods on a cheating husband for one of his clients. Scott now worked as a private investigator.

"No. Actually, I have a pretty good reason for calling you so early," Roger stated. "I saw a very interesting item on the news this morning. Our good buddy Jack Jordan was murdered yesterday morning in Hendersonville, Tennessee," he divulged.

"You're shitting me," Scott declared. He threw his legs over the side of the bed and reached to turn on his bedside lamp. With the click of a circular switch, a 100-watt bulb turned the dark to light. Scott squinted, momentarily blinded, but he was fully awake and alert now.

"No, I'm not shitting you," Roger confirmed, continuing, "The kicker is...are you ready for this...? His throat was slashed."

"Shit!" Scott exclaimed, standing to race across the room. He snatched a pair of jeans from the back of a wooden chair in the corner, leaving the chair tottering back and forth. "What else do you know, Roger? I take it you have talked to the detectives in Hendersonville," he presumed. He held the receiver against his shoulder blade as he used both hands and hopped from leg to leg to pull his jeans over the bulky boxer shorts he had been sleeping in.

"Yes. I had quite a conversation with the detective in Hendersonville assigned to the case – a woman named Sherri Ball. I filled her in on the serial murders that occurred here. The MO of Jack's homicide is the same – slashed throat, knife to the family jewels, and handcuffs...the whole nine yards."

"Crap!" Scott swore again. Taking the phone away from his ear and switching hands, he pulled a slightly soiled T-shirt over his head. "So where do you guys go from here?" he asked as soon as he placed the receiver back to his ear.

"You already know the answer to that, Scott. You were a homicide detective. We sit back and we wait. It's out of our jurisdiction. If Jeanette is caught, then we can have her extradited back to Kentucky to stand trial for the murders she committed here after she is tried for the murder in Tennessee. But it's up to the authorities in Tennessee to prove her connection with Jack's murder and bring her in."

"And I have a feeling that is why you called *me*. Because I don't have to just sit back and wait. It's why I left the force in the first place," Scott reiterated. Roger knew this fact better than anyone.

"I knew you would want to be apprised of this new information. I know you have been searching for Jeanette since you left the force over a year-and-a-half ago, and that all of your leads have gone dry. I thought you might want to follow up on what seems to be a new viable lead. That is…if you can tear yourself away from tracking down all of those cheating husbands and wives," Roger taunted.

"Yeah…you know that'll be a real chore," Scott stated with sarcasm. "I appreciate the call, partner," he affirmed with newfound optimism. "I'm headed to Hendersonville ASAP. And I intend to look up Ms. Ball and pick her brain for what she might know…today and down the road."

"I dropped your name to her, Scott," Roger confessed. "I think she'll be expecting you."

"Thanks, Rog. I owe you big time," Scott said. Catching a glimpse of himself in his dresser mirror, he spit on his hand and rubbed it through his thick, black hair, smoothing down wayward strands. He was in a hurry to leave, so he did not have time to grab a comb. "I'll be in touch, buddy."

"You do that, Scott," Roger said. "Hey…" he said, before Scott had a chance to hang up. "Just watch your back. Okay?"

"Will do," Scott said. And with that, he ended the call.

Scott scooped up a pair of leather athletic shoes from the floor. A pair of socks was shoved inside. He walked back over to the bedside table and laid the phone on the table by its charger base.

Sitting down on the side of the bed, Scott pulled a sock from a shoe. Holding it to his nose, he gave it a quick sniff. He had worn these socks the day before, and he needed to declare them fresh enough for another day's wear.

Finding the socks virtually stench free, Scott covered his feet with them. Then he shoved his athletic shoes on and tied the laces. Standing, he switched off the lamp, turned, and rushed from the room.

Whizzing down the hall, Scott stopped at the entrance to the kitchen, reaching in to flip a wall switch. An overhead dome light bathed the room in light. Propelling his long legs across the room, he grabbed the brass handle of an overhead cabinet. The clasp released with a *click* and the door swung open. Scott reached inside and pulled forth a plastic glass, sitting it with a clunk on the kitchen counter. He pushed the cabinet door closed with a bang.

Whirling around, he grabbed the handle on the refrigerator door, and jerked it open. As Scott leaned inside, extracting a plastic container of milk, cool air met his face and slim body. Unscrewing the top from the milk jug, Scott pulled the container up to his nose. He was relieved to find the milk unspoiled, since he only went to the grocery sporadically.

Stepping around the still-open refrigerator and up to the counter, Scott tipped the milk jug over the glass. White fluid splashed and bubbled inside. He screwed the top back on the container, swiveled around the refrigerator door, and sat it back on a shelf inside. Then he shut the door with a soft clink.

Turning, Scott grabbed a small box of Krispy Creme donuts and his glass of milk from the counter. Shoving the box of donuts under his arm, he snatched his car keys from the kitchen table. The keys jingled in his hand as he headed toward the back door. Opening the door, he took a second to switch off the light in the kitchen, leaving the house dark once more. As he rushed from the house, shutting and locking the door behind him, he silently pledged, *Look out, Jeanette, I'm coming to Tennessee to find you!*

Scott was exhilarated for the first time in a long while.

Chapter 2

Recap

Deputy Sheriff Jack Jordan's murder consumed Jeanette Peterson's mind. She felt an extreme rush each time she mulled over his sadistic death. She had not felt this heavenly since her killing spree in Kentucky over a year ago.

But my life has totally changed since then, she reminded herself, lowering her head into her hands and kneading her forehead. She was sitting on her couch in a darkened living room. A spring day, it was raining cats and dogs outside.

Jeanette had put her homicidal tendencies behind her and started a whole new life in the Nashville area. She even had a new identity she had gone to great pains to steal. *Ghosting, they called it.* She had researched how to assume a dead person's identity, and she had accomplished it step-by-step: new birth certificate, new social security number, new ID. Jeanette was now known as Debbie Gray, a sick tribute to one of the people she had viciously slaughtered in Kentucky.

Jeanette had even radically altered her look. Whereas Jeanette had once donned short, curly, bright auburn hair, Debbie through religious hair color treatments, sported dark black hair instead. And Jeanette allowed Debbie to have much longer hair. Debbie's hair hung past the middle of her back, pulling out much of the natural curl Jeanette's had contained. Debbie's translucent green eyes replaced Jeanette's bright blue ones – compliments of special contact lenses. And lastly, Jeanette had put on about twenty-five pounds, which not only made her body fuller, but her face and neck as well.

Debbie Gray had settled into a peaceful life in Tennessee with her three-year-old daughter, Susanna. Susanna was not Debbie's natural daughter. She had been adopted. Jeanette had killed both of Susanna's parents – her mom first, and later her dad, after a tiring marriage with him.

Jeanette had one other, essential, deep dark secret. She was not a woman, even though outwardly she appeared female. Reifenstein Syndrome was a disorder that had made Jeanette's life a living hell. Born a boy, she always appeared to be a girl. This illness meant her body rejected all male hormones. She had always felt like a boy – playing with boys and enjoying their games. But because she looked like a girl, her parents had forced her to act like one and had been disturbed by her odd, male behavior.

When Jeanette's parents found out about her medical disorder, they refused to accept it. They put her through surgery to remove the useless male genitalia. Doctors actually recommended this procedure, because a high likelihood of testicular cancer loomed if the undeveloped testicles they found remained.

Her parents also approved breast augmentation surgery. They wanted their *daughter* to look like a woman. They believed adding this enhancement would make Jeanette feel like a woman and be able to lead a woman's life. But Jeanette found acting in this manner impossible. She felt like a freak of nature.

As she watched people leading normal lives, Jeanette could not escape the insufferable envy she felt. Killing became an outlet for her frustrations and anger. First, it was merely animals, but eventually, she turned to human prey. Renee – Susanna's mom – had been Jeanette's first human victim. The overall satisfaction, and mock sexual rush, she received led her to commit three more murders in Kentucky, with Mitch – Susanna's dad – being her last.

Feeling heat from police detectives in Kentucky, and collecting $200,000 in life insurance from Mitch, Jeanette fled Kentucky and started a brand new life in Tennessee as Debbie Gray. Debbie Gray's life was free from killing and the desire to kill. At least it had been until now.

And it needs to be again. I need to chase away this craving once more. I'll make an appointment with Dr. Cleaver. He can help me, Debbie tried to convince herself.

She had begun seeing this psychiatrist shortly after moving to Tennessee and his therapy sessions had seemed to help put her homicidal urges to bed. She had to get back on track. Debbie could not allow Jack's bloody slaying to start her on a killing rampage again. She had to find a way to squelch her insane longings to kill some more.

She needed to stop thinking about Jack's death. Hating Jack, Debbie had fantasized about slitting his throat and sinking a knife down low on many occasions, so his death brought extreme pleasure. But now, she needed to rein in these old, familiar, delightful stirrings to kill. Leading a peaceful life in Tennessee and raising her daughter had to take precedence.

Debbie arose from the couch, made her way to her kitchen, picked up the phone, and called Dr. Wallace Cleaver's office. *This madness ends now!*

Chapter 3

Dr. Cleaver

Dr. Wallace Cleaver cradled his bald head in his hands. He had a splitting headache. Unable to focus on the case file on his desk in front of him, he concluded with aggravation, *I need an aspirin.* He had been taking a lot of aspirin over the last two years, since leaving Bowling Green, Kentucky, moving to Nashville, Tennessee, and setting up a private practice.

Wally pulled out his top desk drawer, grimacing as it screeched. *I need to have that drawer oiled*, he reminded himself. He reached inside and pulled forth a bottle of aspirin. He screwed off the lid and tossed the small, white, plastic cap on his desk. It clattered as it settled.

Shaking the container and rattling pills together, he emptied two aspirins into the palm of his hand. Setting the bottle on the top of his leg, he picked up the top and screwed it back in place. As he pitched the container in the drawer, the pills rattled once more as the container landed amongst paper and other items with a dull thud. Wally attempted to quietly push the noisy drawer shut.

Pushing back his high-backed leather chair, he stood and walked over to a small, round table in the corner of the room. On the table were a box of Kleenexes, a clear, plastic pitcher full of ice and water, and three glass tumblers. Wally reached to slide one of the tumblers across the Formica-topped table. A scratching sound had his mouth contorting, and Wally picked up the glass instead.

Wally lifted the pitcher. Even the sound of the ice cubes hitting the glass and the water splashing amongst them caused him distress. He was still grateful to his secretary, Marissa. She took good care of him, keeping fresh ice and water on hand for him all during the day.

Wally popped the aspirins into his mouth, raised the glass, and washed the pills down with a gulp. He sat the glass on the corner of the table. Loosening his tie, unbuttoning his top shirt button, and kicking off his dress shoes, he bypassed the chairs at the table and made his way over to the leather sofa on the other side of the room by the door. The springs groaned as Wally settled his 180-pound frame on the sofa, lying down and stretching out the full length of the couch. Only five-foot-seven, Wally and the couch were a perfect fit.

Wally did not have another appointment for about an hour. *I'll take a little nap and let the aspirin take effect*, he told himself. *Marissa will intercom me when my next patient gets here. Hopefully, by then I will feel much better.* Wally closed his eyes and tried to relax.

* * * *

The intercom buzzed on Dr. Cleaver's desk. Wally was sitting at his desk again now. He reached out and clicked the button on the intercom, "Yes, Marissa?"

"Debbie Gray is here for her three o'clock appointment," she announced.

"Thank you, Marissa," he said. "Send her in."

"Will do," she replied.

Wally watched his office door open and Debbie Gray stroll into his office. He folded his hands over his rounded belly and gave her an exaggerated smile and a nod. "Hello, Debbie," he said.

"Hello, Wally," she replied. There was a neutral expression on her face as she pulled out the chair in front of his desk and had a seat.

Debbie noted that Dr. Cleaver's tie had been loosened and the top button of his shirt was undone. She found this state of affairs strange. Dr. Cleaver was usually neat as a penny.

"Is something wrong, Debbie?" Wally asked, rolling his thumbs.

"I...the fantasies are back again, Dr. Cleaver," she answered, delving right into her reason for being there. *I'm not here to mull over or talk about my doctor's appearance. I'm here for help.*

"Okay. Why don't you tell me a bit about these fantasies then," he suggested, leaning back in his chair and rocking a bit.

"Do I need to go over this *again*?" Debbie asked, shaking her head and gripping the arms of her chair. "You know what I fantasize about. I dream about killing people. About slicing their throats and mutilating their bodies. I thirst for blood."

"Uh-huh," he responded, nodding his head and looking unruffled. "You haven't been to see me in quite a while, Debbie. I'm assuming that means your violent fantasies have been at bay. What has happened to bring them to life again?"

Instead of answering, Debbie stood and walked over to the table in the corner. Looking down, she spied a pair of men's dress shoes on the floor. *Does he have his shoes off too?* she wondered, surprised anew by her doctor's casual nature this afternoon.

She spied a glass of water sitting on the corner of the table, sweating. She reached and picked out a clean glass. Then she picked up the pitcher and poured some water for herself, holding the glass away from her to keep from being splashed by the ice pouring out of the pitcher with the liquid.

Instead of going back over to Dr. Cleaver's desk, she pulled out a chair from the table and sat with her back to a window. Closed mini-blinds kept the afternoon sun from streaming in, but its warmth felt good on Debbie's back. Debbie looked over at Dr. Cleaver and noted his eyes studying her as he waited for an answer to his last question.

She raised her glass and took a few swallows before she spoke again. "Did you hear about the retired Kentucky deputy sheriff who was murdered at Old Hickory Lake yesterday?" she dared to ask, fighting to remain nonchalant. She wanted to smile. She sat her glass on the table and toyed with it, running her finger around the rim.

"Yes, I did," Wally answered. Sitting up straight in his chair, he swiveled it back and forth, asking, "What has that got to do with anything, Debbie? Does the brutality of his murder excite you?"

"You know that it does," Debbie confessed. Her hand shook as she took another drink of water. "And there is something else, doc. This man's murder *especially* excites me. Do you want to know why? No…don't answer that," she said. "I already know that you do."

"So why don't you tell me then?" Wally suggested, sinking back down in his chair again. He laid his hands on his stomach once more, but his index fingers were pointing out at Debbie, as if to say, 'Your turn'.

"That's what I'm here for…to talk," she commented, a hostile edge to her voice. She raised her glass again and rolled it in her hands.

"Then why don't you just do that?" Wally asked. Glancing at his watch, and looking bored, he reminded her, "Your session is only twenty minutes. If you want my help, I would strongly suggest you tell me what you are feeling, so I can offer some suggestions. But it's your dime. If all you want to do is play games…"

"You think I'm playing games?" she growled. Her glass clattered on the table as she lowered it a bit harder than she had intended. She leapt to her feet and walked over to the chair in front of his desk. Squeezing the back, she asked, "Tell me, Wally, do you think Jack Jordan thought his killer was playing games when they slit his throat or when they sliced off his dick? Would you think I was playing games if I did that to you?"

"Oh...now we are getting somewhere," he commented, daring to smile. He had also sat up straight in his chair and was tapping his hands on the arms. "It's your anger that drives these fantasies, Debbie. If you get the anger out...in a productive way...the fantasies will diminish and eventually go away again."

"In a productive way, huh?" she questioned with a chuckle.

Debbie released the top of the chair, walked around it, sauntered up to the doctor's desk, and in the blink of an eye, snatched up a heavy, golden letter opener. Holding it up in front of her, she ran her finger along the sharp tip. "But what if what I find productive and what you find productive are two different things, Wally? For instance...what if what I find productive is jamming this letter opener into your throat and watching you bleed out like Jack Jordan?"

Wally hands had stilled. He was gripping the arms of his chair and his eyes were fixated on Debbie and the letter opener. He did not look scared though. "You never did tell me why Deputy Sheriff Jack Jordan's death excites you so much, Debbie," he continued right where he left off, totally ignoring Debbie's threat.

Debbie sat down in the chair in front of Dr. Cleaver's desk. She held the letter opener perpendicular, almost at chin level, twisting it between in her hands. A second later, she bent forward and dropped the letter opener – point down – into a pencil holder on the doctor's desk. It made a ringing sound as it settled.

"You'd be no fun to kill," she told him with a half-smirk. "The fun of killing is the fear in their eyes."

"If you say so," he commented, tapping his fingers again. "Do you suppose Jack Jordan had fear in his eyes?"

"You're determined to talk about Jack Jordan; aren't you, doc?" Debbie asked, sitting back in her chair and relaxing a bit. The doctor was right. Her last burst of anger had calmed her, and she had not really hurt him.

"You brought him up – not me," he reminded her.

"Yeah, I did. Didn't I?" she said. "I knew Jack Jordan," she confessed, picking at her nail polish. She hated the stuff, but she wore it because it made her look more feminine.

"But he obviously wasn't a friend of yours. Otherwise, I can't imagine that you would be thrilled by his murder," the doctor stated, folding his hands again.

"No. He wasn't a friend. Far from it. I hated his guts," she admitted, grinding her teeth.

"And did you fantasize about killing this man?" he questioned, swinging his chair again.

"On numerous occasions. Exactly the same way that he died," she dared to divulge, one corner of her mouth curving up.

"So no wonder his death gives you such a thrill then," the doctor concluded. "Your fantasy has been fulfilled," he pointed out, stilling his chair and pointing his index fingers at her.

"Police are looking for Jack Jordan's killer, Wally," Debbie reminded him. "So what makes you so certain I didn't fulfill my fantasy and kill him?" she asked, leaning forward and glaring at him with evil green eyes.

"Are you telling me you did?" Dr. Cleaver had the nerve to ask, meeting her steely glare with hard eyes of his own.

There was dead silence in the room for several moments as the two continued to stare one another down. Finally Debbie broke the silence, asking, "What if I told you I did? Would you turn me in to the cops? Or would doctor-patient confidentiality come into play?"

"This is the twenty-first century, Debbie," Dr. Cleaver reminded her. "In today's legal system, a danger to society cancels out doctor-patient confidentiality."

"Are you saying I'm a danger to society?" she questioned with an amused smile and chuckle.

"If you are going around slitting men's throats and neutering them, then I would say...yes...you are a definite danger to society. What would you say?" he asked, returning her smile as if they were playing a game with one another.

"You don't really believe I killed him, do you?" she inquired, relaxing back in her chair again.

"I know you didn't," Debbie was surprised to hear the doctor answer with confidence. "Fantasy can sometimes seem like reality. This crime hits home with what you dream of doing, so it's only natural that it excites you. It's also quite natural that you would interject yourself into the crime as the killer. Isn't that really what's going on here, Debbie?"

"You're the doctor. You should know," she replied, giving him another grin.

"Yes. I should," he agreed. He looked down at his watch again.

"Is my time up?" Debbie asked.

"Just about," he answered. "I'd like to see you again, Debbie. I think you need to work through your anger in order to chase away these fantasies and delusions you are experiencing. Could you come in to see me again...?" He paused and thumbed through a calendar on his desk. "...Tomorrow? Same time?" he suggested.

"Tomorrow. Same time," she agreed, standing and walking toward the door.

Debbie rather enjoyed her therapy sessions with Dr. Cleaver. He was no nonsense and he seemed to have no fear. He had no idea what real danger he was in, and she had no intention of confessing to anything either.

"See you tomorrow, Wally," Debbie said, as she placed her hand on the doorknob. "Good therapy session."

"Yes. I think it was," he agreed, giving her the same lopsided grin he had donned when she walked in.

SISSY MARLYN

Debbie opened the door and walked out. Her therapy session was over, and she felt calmer. *If nothing else, the games are fun.* She already looked forward to tomorrow's session.

Chapter 4

Private Investigation

Scott pulled his blue Econoline van into the parking lot of the Hendersonville Police Department on Executive Drive. This visit was his second of the day. When he left Louisville, bright and early that morning, he had not thought to call the Hendersonville PD and ask when Detective Ball would be in. When he had arrived that morning, he had been told she was working the evening shift and would not be in until 6:00 p.m.

Scott had spent the day nosing around and killing time. He had gone to Old Hickory Lake and walked around the crime scene, in the rain, careful not to disturb anything. He had even taken some long-range photographs of the murder site from the back of his surveillance van. His camera was always close at hand – an essential item for PI work.

It was 6:00 p.m. now. Scott grabbed a light nylon jacket from his passenger seat. He usually had one tossed somewhere in the van. Springtime temperatures sometime got rather nippy late at night when he was doing surveillance for some case.

Vacating his van, Scott slipped his jacket on and zipped it – to hide his soiled shirt. His shirt had pizza stains down the front – one of his popular staples of late. Scott did not want to go into the police station looking like a slob.

He thought of how neat and orderly he used to dress when he had been a Metro Louisville homicide detective. He had let a lot of things slide since leaving the force – the most essential being his appearance. He reached for and fingered the dark, three-day stubble on his chin and above his upper lip.

Allowing his long, spindly legs to propel him toward the front door of the two-story, brick police building, Scott squinted into the low evening sun as it broke through the clouds. He also watched, and listened, to the American flag flapping in the breeze. Reaching the glass front door, Scott pulled it open and stepped into the police station.

The lobby was dimly lit and quiet. No one else walked about this area at this moment. Scott walked across several throw rugs, one with the police emblem on it, and passed some elevators. He approached the information desk a few feet ahead of him.

An officer in uniform sat behind the green Formica-topped desk. There was a large American flag on the wall behind him. "Can I help you?" this officer asked, staring at Scott's face with steely blue eyes.

"Is Detective Sherri Ball in?" Scott inquired.

"Is she expectin' you? Do you have an appointment with her?" the man questioned, eyeballing him for head to foot, as if he were some derelict.

"Um...actually...I left my name here this morning with the other officer who was at this desk," Scott informed him. "My name is Scott Arnold."

"Okay, Mr. Arnold," the man said. Turning his head and picking up a phone, he told him, "I'll just call Sergeant Ball and see if she would like to meet with you."

"That'd be great. Thanks," Scott said, giving the officer an icebreaking smile.

Scott lightly drummed his fingers on the counter as he watched the man punch in Detective Ball's extension. Scott just hoped Roger dropping his name garnered him a meeting with this woman. He was eager to gather all the facts about Jack Jordan's murder.

"Sergeant Ball," Scott heard the officer say. "There is a Scott...*Ar...nold* here to see you." The man glanced back up at him. Scott waited anxiously through a silent pause. "Okay," he heard the officer reply. He lowered the receiver. Staring at

Scott with eyes that seemed to say, 'I don't know why…but…', the man told Scott, "Sergeant Ball *will* see you. Take the elevator to the second floor; she'll meet you there." He pointed in the direction of the elevators.

"Thanks. That I'll do," Scott said, showing straight, white teeth. The officer had already dismissed him, studying something on his desk. Scott turned and skipped off toward the elevator. *Thanks, Roger*, Scott also thought.

When the elevator doors clanged opened on the second floor, Scott spied a woman standing across the hall by a closed door. She was dressed in a shiny ivory blouse, silky black dress slacks and blazer and low-heeled pumps. Her straight, shoulder-length, dark brown hair showcased her deep chocolate eyes and unblemished, healthy glowing skin.

As Scott stepped off the elevator, this woman took a step toward him. "Scott Arnold?" she asked, her wide, ruby lips arching into a smile.

"Yes," Scott answered, closing the space between them. Offering his hand, he said, "And you must be Sergeant Ball."

"That I am," she revealed, linking her hand with his for a firm handshake. "Welcome to Hendersonvill', Mr. Arnold. I understand from your ex-partner at Louisvill' homicide that you are interested in the details of the Jack Jordan homicide."

"Very much so," Scott concurred, nodding his head and releasing her hand.

He immediately noted two things about Detective Sherri Ball: her strong, yet charming, southern accent and the scent of her perfume. Detective Ball's perfume reminded him of the fragrance his deceased girlfriend, Debbie, used to wear. As usual, when he thought of his beloved Debbie, Scott still felt an ache in his heart.

Backing away from Sergeant Ball, Scott sunk his hands into the pockets of his jacket. "Could we go to your office and talk?" he asked, breaking eye contact and toeing the gray linoleum floor.

"Well…my office isn't the most private place in the world," Detective Ball said with a chuckle. "It's a small area and the desks are side by side."

"Similar to Louisville," Scott commented with a reminiscent snigger, glancing up at her again.

"Probably…I imagine…but a bit smaller," she clarified, giving him another friendly smile.

"So where can we talk?" Scott probed, rocking on his heel. He was anxious to hear whatever information she could share.

"There's a conference room down the hall. How about I take us there?"

"I'll be right beside you," Scott agreed.

Detective Ball nodded, turned, and began walking down the hall. Scott checked his pace and walked in step with her. Sherri was only about five-five, and Scott was over six foot tall. If Scott walked at a normal pace, his long legs would have propelled him far in front of Sergeant Ball.

The two were silent as they walked down the short, dimly lit hall. No one else lingered in the hallway, and the few doors they passed were closed. The only sound was the noise of their feet shuffling on the tile floor.

Sherri came to a small conference room. She opened the door, reached inside, and flipped a light switch. Fluorescent lights flickered and glowed overhead. A small table, with four, black, aluminum-framed chairs, sat in the center of the room. On the paneled wall facing them hung a white, dry erase board. The other four walls were bare.

"Almost looks like an interrogation room," Scott commented with a snicker.

"Actually, we have used it for that on occasion, when our real investigation room is full," Sherri admitted. "Which…isn't too often. Hendersonvill' is a pretty peaceful town. That is…until Jack Jordan's grisly homicide. If you guys have information to share with us, to help us catch the perp in this case, then I'm just as anxious to talk to you as you are to talk to me," she confessed.

Scott nodded and smiled. He liked listening to Detective Ball's southern drawl. *It's cute*, he found himself thinking.

Scott broke eye contact with Sherri and made his way into the conference room. Sherri pulled the door shut and also entered the room. The metal-framed chairs made screeching noises on the tile floor as both Scott and Detective Ball slid them out from the table, sat down, and repositioned them closer to the table once more. Sherri faced Scott, who sat directly across the table. The dry erase board, directly behind him, framed his head. It brought extra emphasis to Scott's jet-black hair and dark brown – almost black – eyes.

"Soo..." Detective Ball spoke again, comfortably placing her arms on the table and one hand on top of the other. She noticed an amused smile appear on Scott's face. "What?" she asked, her eyes puzzled.

"Nothing," he chuckled. "It's just...I...I like your accent," he confessed. "You draw out your vowels...s*oooo*," he mimicked, snickering again.

"*Oh...*," she commented and returned his smile. "And I thought it was you that had the accent. That northern brogue."

"Point well taken," Scott agreed, nodding his head and chuckling some more. He settled back into his chair. He found Sherri to be very personable and easy to talk to. He hoped their exchange of information came as easy. "Well, obviously, I didn't come here to discuss differences in our speech patterns." He got right to the point. "I need to know what you guys found out in your investigation so far of Jack Jordan's homicide," .

"Do you mind if I ask why you are so interested in this case?" Sherri asked, tapping her fingers on the top of her hand. "I understand from your ex-partner that you were the homicide detective on similar unsolved murders in Louisvill', but you're a PI now. What bearin' does this homicide have on your new career?"

"I wouldn't exactly call being a PI a career," Scott clarified with a smirk and a guffaw. He leaned back in his chair and stuck his hands in the pockets of his jacket. "I left the force to further investigate the Louisville homicides as a private citizen...one not tied to the rules and regulations of the Metro Louisville Police Department. When my leads all ran dry and my savings account dwindled to nothing, I had to do something to make a living, so becoming a private investigator just fit. But I haven't given up on trying to track down the killer from the Louisville cases. Tracking down cheating spouses and proving insurance fraud is not something I live to do, but it's a necessary evil to keep food on the table and utility bills paid."

"Why are solvin' these murders so important to you?" Sherri continued to question.

Scott reared back in the chair a bit harder, bringing the front legs slightly off the floor. He rocked the chair, tapping the front legs on the floor for a few moments. Then, sitting back up straight in the chair, he made full eye contact with Detective Ball and replied, "Because one of the killer's victims, Debbie Gray, was someone very near and dear to my heart, and I want to make sure Jeanette Peterson is caught and punished for what she has done."

"Ah...you mentioned a precise perp's name. So that must mean Louisvill' Metro has effective evidence to prove that this woman...this Jeanette Peterson...is the killer."

"They do," Scott answered with authority. "Oh...and just to clarify things...Jeanette is *not* a woman. Granted, he has a woman's name and identity, and he looks like a woman, but his DNA tells a different story. And Jeanette's *male* DNA was found at two of the crime scenes. In fact, this DNA evidence provided enough reasonable doubt to allow our first suspect, actually arrested for one of the homicides, to go free." Scott had been relieved by this outcome. They had gathered quite a case against an upstanding young woman named Stacy Prescott, before evidence to prove Jeanette's guilt came to light.

"Wow!" Sherri exclaimed, exhaling. "This one certainly sounds complicated."

"You mean the case or Jeanette? If you mean Jeanette, she isn't complicated. She's a devious fraud and a sociopath. And when she fled Louisville over a year and a half ago, she had an eighteen-month-old baby girl with her. To the best of my knowledge, the girl is still alive. One more reason to track down this monster ASAP," Scott said, gnashing his teeth. He also popped his knuckles.

"I'd say," Sherri agreed. "I have a young daughter of my own."

"Married?" Scott found himself asking. He also glanced at her left hand. She was not wearing a ring.

"No…divorced," she answered, averting her eyes for a moment. But before they broke eye contact, Scott caught a glimpse of pain in her eyes. "Anyway…" she continued. "We aren't here to talk about our personal lives. We're here to share information, and now that you've shared information with me, I'll be glad to share some with you."

"Good," Scott said, smiling for the first time in several moments. "What can you tell me about the homicide?"

Sherry looked him in the eye and relayed, "What we know so far is that Jack Jordan succumbed from a lethal injury to the carotid artery in the neck. It appears from the way his neck was hyper-extended that his attacker surprised him from behind. There was no sign of a struggle, because Jack Jordan never got a chance to fight. The injury to his genitals was postmortem. It also appears that the perp handcuffed the victim after he was deceased," she matter-of-factly relayed.

Scott's brow puckered and he raised a fisted hand to his mouth and tapped his knuckle against his lips. He was mulling over all that Detective Ball had shared with him. "So he was attacked from behind and the handcuffs were put on *after* the murder," he mumbled in repetition.

"That's correct," Sherri clarified. "What are your thoughts?"

"My thoughts are…the MO's the same…but yet…different," he replied, rubbing his thumb across the stubble on his chin.

"What do you mean?" Sherri asked, her eyes attentive and inquisitive.

"We had four murders in Kentucky. All of them involved handcuffs; two of them involved fatal wounds to the carotid; three of them involved genitals being mutilated. In fact, in the last two murders, Jeanette left the knife stuck in the genital region."

"As it was in Jack Jordan's," Sherri volunteered. "So what exactly is different?"

"The difference is…Jeanette handcuffed the victims *before* he murdered them. And I believe he deceived each victim into trusting him and then thrilled at watching them die face to face. Of course, with Jack, Jeanette never could have fooled him into trusting him. Jack hated Jeanette and even believed he was our killer. So maybe Jeanette saw his only opportunity to take Jack out being to sneak up on him. It's different, but it's still his style. I suppose the thrill with Jack was in settling an old score and not the fear factor."

"*Or*…" Sherri said, running her hands along the side of her head and gathering them in the back of her hair. "This could be a different killer. Maybe it's a copycat of your Louisvill' killer."

"Well, there's one clear way to find out. Were you guys able to gather any DNA evidence?" Scott questioned.

"So far the only evidence we've gathered were some bloody shoe prints, on the dock and in the dirt leadin' into the woods," she admitted. Fanning her hair out as she releasing her head, she dropped her hands into her waist, leaned forward a bit, and added, "Our evidence techs are workin' on castin' a mould. The knife handle appeared to have been wiped clean and evidently the perp was wearin' gloves."

"Damn," Scott swore, rapping his knuckles against the edge of the table. "Jeanette is very smart. We picked up some

DNA evidence at two of our crimes – strands of her hair – but by and large, she left us little to go on. If this is her – and I believe it is – this will probably only be her first murder. She's a serial killer. She's unleashed her thirst for blood again, so it won't be long before she kills again. Can you keep me in the loop on this investigation, and any similar homicides that might occur in the area?" Scott asked.

His chair screeched as he pushed it back. Rising up out of his chair, he pulled forth his wallet from his back pocket. Unfolding it, he extracted one of his business cards. "This is my contact information…cell phone…home phone…," he said, holding the card out across the table toward Detective Ball.

Sherri reached and took his card. Glancing at it, she said, "Mr. Arnold, I appreciate you comin' here today and sharin' information you believe relates to this case. I will keep you in the loop," she seemed to promise.

"I'll hold you to that," Scott told her, sticking his wallet back into the pocket of his jeans.

There was screeching in the room again as Sherri pushed back her chair and stood. Sherri put Scott's card in her pocket. They both walked to the door. Sherri reached to turn the knob. After Scott had walked past her and out into the hallway, Sherri flipped the light switch. The fluorescent lights flickered to dark, and Sherri pulled the door to the conference room closed.

A door up the hall opened, and a tall, older gentleman in a suit stepped into the hallway. Shutting the door behind him, he smiled and waved in Sherri's direction before heading off down the hall. Sherri waved back. Then she focused her attention back on Scott. "Are you headed back to Louisvill' this evenin'?" she asked.

"Yeah," he answered. They were slowly meandering up the hallway toward the elevators and the door to Sherri's office.

"Well…you have a safe trip home then," she said. "I'm on duty until the early mornin' hours."

"Yeah...I remember those night shifts," Scott reminisced with a laugh.

"Bet you're glad they are only a memory now, huh?" Sherri said with a giggle.

"Not really. Now, my nightshifts are sitting in the dark on some vacant city street getting the goods on some cheating wife or husband. I think I'd rather be doing your form of night shift again."

"Then maybe you should be," Sherri said, looking him straight in the eye. "Maybe you should go back on the police force. Have you thought about it?" she dared to ask.

"*Oh*...yeah," Scott confirmed. "But I want to find Jeanette first." Sinking his hands into his jacket pockets and looking down at his shoes and the linoleum tile, he added in a quieter voice, "I owe that to Debbie's memory."

Sherri felt her heart twist. *He seems like he loved this 'Debbie' a great deal.* She was touched by Scott's devotion and his dedication to finding her killer and seeing that justice was done. "I'll do whatever I can to help you accomplish your goal," Sherri found herself promising as they reached the elevators.

Scott looked up and made eye contact with her. Her eyes relayed sincerity. "Thank you," he said, his lips curving. "I appreciate your time, Detective Ball."

"No problem," she said. "We're on the same side here, Scott. Hendersonvill' is a n*i*ce place to live...and work. I want to see it stays that way," she told him.

"N*iiii*ce...huh?" he teased, mocking her drawl with dancing eyes and a wide smile.

"Time for you to go back to Louisvill', Yankee," Sherri told him, lightly swatting his arm and returning his smile. "You do want to stay on a friendly basis with me, right?" she teased.

"You bet I do," he declared with a chuckle, pressing the elevator button. "You take care. I look forward to hearing from you when you get back all the forensics on the case."

"I'll let you know if we find anythin' that ties into your Louisvill' homicides," Sherri told him.

The elevator doors opened, and Scott stepped aboard. Turning to face Sherry once more, he pressed a silver embossed *1* button. As a white light silhouetted the edges of the *1*, he smiled and waved to Sherri. He briefly saw her grin and her hand wave before the doors clinked closed.

The elevator cable squeaked and groaned as the elevator lowered. Deep in thought, Scott was oblivious to the noise. *I like Detective Ball. She seems very genuine. I think I can depend on her help. This has got to be the lead I'm looking for.*

A single 'ding' and the elevator doors clanging open roused Scott from his contemplation. He vacated the elevator and headed toward the front door of the police station. He passed a few officers in uniform, but since he did not personally know them, he walked on without acknowledging them.

Scott hurried out the front door and into the parking lot, anxious to be on his way. He rushed over to his van and climbed inside, feeling exhilarated for the second time that day. He looked forward to the drive home, alone in the van with just his thoughts, and possibly his first lead to finding Jeanette in a very long time.

Chapter 5

Repartee

Debbie Gray walked into Dr. Cleaver's office right on time the next day. She observed that he was back to his old self. His crisp, Oxford dress shirt was fully buttoned and his tie was perfectly knotted at his neck. She glanced at the floor, across the room by the table, and noted there were no shoes resting there today. *I guess he's wearing shoes today as well*, she assumed, a smile on her face. She pulled out the chair in front of his desk and had a seat.

"Hello, Debbie. What brings you in to see me today?" Dr. Cleaver asked.

He observed she was dressed in her security uniform – a white shirt with a patch on the shoulder reading Gaylord Entertainment Center Security, a navy tie, tan slacks, and black uniform shoes. Debbie also had her black hair pulled back in a ponytail.

"What brings me in?" she asked, a puzzled tone to her voice. "Um…I'd say your request from yesterday brings me in," she clarified, giving him a hard stare.

"Oh…I see," he said, tapping his index fingers on his chin. His eyes darted from side to side, as if he was trying to process new information.

"So exactly what kind of game are we playing today, Wally? Is there some reason you want me to rehash what happened in yesterday's therapy session?" Debbie questioned, pushing her chunky frame up straight in her seat. Her green eyes were stern.

"Perhaps that's precisely what I would like to do," he answered. His top desk drawer screeched as he slid it open. He scratched around inside, sounding like a squirrel pawing through fallen leaves as it searched for nuts. Finally, Dr. Cleaver pulled forth a notepad and pushed the drawer closed with a soft bang. Rattling pens and pencils together, he selected, and extracted, a rollerball pen from the pencil holder on his desk.

"What are you going to do? Take notes?" Debbie probed, disturbed by his commotion and odd behavior. "I wouldn't think yesterday would have been all that forgettable. What, is it *every day* that one of your patients threatens to stab you in the throat with your letter opener?"

Dr. Cleaver's eyes followed the path of Debbie's. They were both staring at the handle of his heavy, gold letter opener, which rested – point down – in the pencil holder on his desk. Dr. Cleaver cleared his throat and squirmed in his chair. Then staring Debbie down, he said, "No, fortunately, that kind of thing doesn't happen every day, Debbie. That's why I'd like to talk about this incident some more. Why exactly did you feel the need to threaten me?"

"I didn't threaten you, Wally. I don't make idle threats. If I had truly wanted to hurt you, you wouldn't be sitting here today," Debbie said, gnashing her teeth.

"Is that so? You're that dangerous, huh?" he challenged, sitting up straight in his seat and squeezing his pen between his hands.

"If you only knew," she replied, a crooked smirk on her face.

"That's just the point," he said, shaking his pen at her. "I need to know, Debbie. Are the homicidal fantasies back? Is that why you are so fixated on doing me harm with my letter opener?"

"You know they are. I told you that yesterday," she growled. Her eyes narrowed and pierced.

"You did...didn't you," Dr. Cleaver stated, clicking the pen and jotting something down on his notepad.

"Why the note-taking today?" Debbie asked, leaning forward in her chair and trying to read what he had written. Dr. Cleaver snatched up the notepad and held it at his waist, facing away from her. "Why are you hiding what you wrote, Wally? What's the big secret?" Debbie questioned, a hostile edge to her voice.

"I always take notes of our sessions, Debbie. I usually do my reports after your session ends. But today, I have another patient right afterwards, so I'm taking notes as we go," he explained, holding his pen up in the air. "Why should that bother you?"

"It's just different...that's all," she stated, staring at the cardboard back of the notepad.

"If it bothers you, I'll put the pad away," Dr. Cleaver told her, shifting his pen to the other hand and opening back up his squeaky top drawer.

"Take notes. I could give a rat's ass!" Debbie exclaimed, flinging her hand downward and dismissing him. She slid back her chair, stood and walked across the room. She strolled over to the window. Grabbing a small plastic handle and twisting it, she opened the mini-blinds, letting in the bright, afternoon sunshine. "You like the darkness. Don't you, Wally?" she asked, turning to face him again.

Blinking and squinting at the sudden brightness in the room, he confessed, "Sometimes I get headaches and the light hurts my eyes."

"Well...if you have chronic headaches, you should probably see a doctor," Debbie taunted him. She twisted the handle on the mini-blinds again, darkening the room once more. "I like to hide in the dark too," she said with a chuckle.

"What are you hiding from, Debbie?" he asked, picking up on her last thought. He pushed his drawer back shut, laid the notepad back on the desk face down, and twisted his pen in his hands.

"I hide from myself. From the evil inside," she told him, releasing the blind cable with a jerk.

"I see," Dr. Cleaver commented, tapping his pen on his bottom lip.

"Do you?" Debbie challenged, walking back over toward his desk. "What exactly do you see, Wally?" she asked. She stood in front of him, with her hands on her hips, staring through him.

"I think we've already been over this in other therapy sessions, Debbie," he replied, tossing his pen with a plop on top of his notepad. "You had a bad childhood. So you are displacing anger at your parents. I don't know what has set this off again…"

"What do you mean you don't know?" she asked, placing her hands on the edge of his desk and leaning in toward him. "I told you yesterday that it was Jack Jordan's murder," she hissed.

Dr. Cleaver leaned back in his chair, gripping the ends and tapping his fingers. "O…kay," he replied. "Let's talk about Jack's murder."

"Why are we going in circles?" she probed, releasing his desk and pacing the room. "I told you yesterday that Jack Jordan's death excites me because I hated him and always fantasized about killing him. You said I'm – what was it? – transposing myself into the violence of his murder. Thus, fulfilling my fantasy. Or some such shit. Right?"

"Sounds right," he responded, picking up his pen, turning over the notepad, and scribbling a few more notes. Looking back up at Debbie, he suggested, "Why don't we discuss your relationship with Jack Jordan more, Debbie? Can we do that?"

"Back to Jack Jordan again!" she spewed. The cushion in the chair in front of Dr. Cleaver's desk made a poofing sound as Debbie flopped down into it. "If you really must know…Jack and I had sex a few times, so he thought he owned me. He was in my face every time I turned around when I lived in Kentucky. He was an ugly, bugged-eyed, old man, and he deserved to die. Is that enough about our relationship?"

"I hear a lot of anger when you speak of him, Debbie," Dr. Cleaver pointed out, twirling his pen in his hands. "Must make you feel good that someone did him in in such a violent manner."

"I told you that it does," she said. "Why do I feel like this therapy session is a repeat of yesterday?"

"It's a continuation of yesterday," Dr. Cleaver clarified, shaking his pen at her. Then he immediately shot another question at Debbie. "Would you describe Jack Jordan as a bully?"

"Oh, yeah! Big time!" she agreed, nodding her head.

"And your parents pretty much bullied you too, didn't they?" He cleverly tied the two together.

"I guess. They forced me to do things I didn't want to," she admitted, rocking in her chair and tapping her thumbs together. Her lips were pursed.

"And you are a much better parent to your little girl, right?" he asked, laying his pen back on his notepad.

"Definitely!" Debbie declared with confidence, sitting up in her chair and nodding her head.

"That little girl is the most important thing in the world to you, isn't she?"

"You know that she is," she professed.

"Then…as we've discussed before…you must keep your anger under control…"

"That's why I'm here," she acknowledged, squeezing the arms of her chair.

"I know it is, Debbie," Dr. Cleaver concurred, pulling on the side of his mustache. "It all comes down to choices. Either you put your little girl first, or you lose yourself to your violent fantasies. Jack Jordan is dead. He can't bully you anymore, so he needs to be put out of your thoughts. Your sole focus needs to be your daughter and your life with her. Are we agreed?"

Debbie was silent for a moment, picking at her thumbnail. Then she looked Dr. Cleaver in the eye and agreed. "Yes. Susanna and her welfare come first. To hell with Jack Jordan! I truly hope that is where he now resides."

"When the violent fantasies rear their head, you need to think of your daughter and her welfare. That's what I advised you before, and I assume it has worked, because I haven't seen you in a while," Dr. Cleaver commented with a smile.

"Until yesterday," Debbie reminded him.

"Yes...that's right. Until yesterday," he agreed, tapping a fist to his bottom lip. He glanced at his watch and said, "I think this has been a good therapy session. How do you feel?"

"I agree," Debbie said, giving him a smile. "I don't know how you do it, doc. But you manage to calm the demons within me. I appreciate it a great deal."

"That's what I get paid the big bucks for," he said with a chuckle. "Why don't you see Marissa, and set up another appointment for next month. Just to check in. How does that sound?"

"Reasonable. After all, I don't get paid the *big* bucks where I work," she said with a snicker, as she rose from her chair. "Thanks, Wally."

"Take care, Debbie. Give Susanna a hug for me," he said.

"That I will do," she said as she walked over to the door and opened it.

When Debbie had stepped out and shut the door, Dr. Cleaver leaned back in his chair. He rubbed his chin and stared at his framed and matted medical certificate on the wall across the room. Picking up the notepad from his desk, he studied his notes.

Wally shuddered as he accepted that he had not remembered yesterday's session with Debbie at all. This was not the first time his severe headaches had left him with memory lapses. He did not like these odd occurrences one bit. He considered Debbie's advice. *Maybe I should see a doctor about my headaches*, he pondered.

"I'll worry about this later," he said aloud, as he opened a bottom desk drawer, thumbed through several file folders, located Debbie's, and pulled it out.

As he had told her, he needed to make some notes on today's session for future reference. He tore off the top page of his notepad and began recording the details of his current therapy session with Debbie, beginning at the top with the date. He would put this report away in her file and study his notes before her next therapy session.

Dr. Cleaver was confident there would be more therapy sessions with Debbie. She held a deep-seated anger toward her parents, and this issue had yet to be resolved. Until she fully came to terms with her anger, the ugly head of violence would again and again rear itself in Debbie's life.

Regardless of these facts, Dr. Cleaver did not consider Debbie to be any real threat to anyone. He was glad he could help her put her aggressive fantasies aside and live a happy life with her little girl. Helping people was why he had become a psychiatrist in the first place. He believed that everyone needed to come to terms with their past and then they could lead a healthy, full life. He had helped so many in the past, and he planned to help that many more in the future. *No one will ever stop me from doing what I love*, Wally contemplated. He was not going to let a few memory lapses here and there get in the way.

Chapter 6

Homicidal Tendencies

Savage Pride had just finished a concert at the Gaylord Entertainment Center in Nashville. Mason Greathouse, the band's lead singer and teen heartthrob, had just exited the arena, stepping into a private, darkened dock area in back of the auditorium. Hot from being under extensive lighting and gyrating on stage for almost two hours, Mason savored the unheated dock. Cool air caressed his face and body.

Mason looked across the way and spotted four lit-up motor coaches. He could hear the engines running and smell the diesel. One of these buses was his and his family's. He headed across the concrete pavement toward his tour coach, knowing his wife and young daughter awaited him.

"Hey, Mas, hold up a second," he heard his friend and keyboard player, Robert, call.

Mason stopped and turned his head. He heard the exit door shut and saw Robert walking toward him. He waited for him to approach. "What's up?" he asked.

"Nothing. Great concert tonight, huh?" Robert said with a smile, sinking his hands into the pockets of his jeans.

"Yep," Mason agreed. "Is that all you wanted to do was congratulate me?" he chuckled.

"No," Robert snickered. "I was just wondering if you wanted to hang with me, go crash some honky-tonks on Broadway, get some bar chow, and maybe check out a band or two? I'm starving, and I'm keyed up from the concert. How about you? The rest of the guys already left…with groupies."

"Let me go check in with Callie and see how Sarah's doing. If we can get someone to baby-sit for a few hours, then maybe Callie can go into NashVegas with us. I know she gets tired of being cramped up on the bus all the time."

"Sounds like a plan. I'll go change shirts. This one's a little sweaty. I'll come knock on your door in a few."

"Alright. Sounds good," Mason agreed.

The two friends parted and walked off in different directions, each going to their respective bus.

* * * *

Mason's wife, Callie, decided not to go into town with Mason and Robert. Three-year-old Sarah had been a bit fussy that evening, and she had had a hard time getting the little girl to sleep, so Callie was tired. She gave Mason her blessing to go into town with Robert though. She knew the guys were always keyed up after a concert. So Mason and Robert donned cowboy hats and dark glasses and headed onto the NashVegas strip to have some fun. Two plainclothes security men went into town with them. One male and one female security officer remained behind to guard over the two motor coaches. The female security guard was Debbie Gray.

* * * *

Robert, true-to-form, found a woman to keep him company shortly after hitting the honky-tonks. He and Mason – tall men with thick, shoulder-length, black hair and engaging golden brown eyes – naturally attracted attention from the opposite sex. But since Mason was happily married, and did not wish any other female companionship, he parted company with Robert.

Robert's security guy sat on a barstool, bored, as he drank Coca-Cola and watched from a distance through the smoky haze over Robert and his new girlfriend. He also watched the band – four men in cowboy hats, western shirts and jeans performing county classics, which he liked. Currently, they sang Willie Nelson's "On The Road Again".

Mason and his security guy were on the move. They weaved through people on Broadway. Restaurants, interspersed on the strip, released delectable scents, leaving their mouths watering. A variety of live music streamed from each honky-tonk they passed. One club offered blues, another modern country, another classical country, and one even had karaoke. Signs and buildings lined in neon bathed the avenue in a kaleidoscope of color. Mason ducked in a few bars to check out the up-and-coming bands. His security guard fought to stay in tow, squeezing through throngs of people.

* * * *

Early morning, about 1:20 a.m.: One of Savage Pride's 'cowboys' had finally had enough of Nashville nightlife. Relishing the quiet and solitude, he made his way around the far side of the entertainment center and headed back to his tour bus for the night. He had no idea he was being pursued.

His follower tried to keep his footsteps light as he slowly closed the distance between them. *Maybe he'll think I'm his security guard,* he thought. The singing sensation's pursuer had been relieved when this man's real security guard had gotten separated from his charge somewhere in one of the crowds.

Fully around the corner now, the street was still bright from ample street lights, and police cars lined the avenue. There was a police substation in front of the Gaylord. However, the cowboy and his pursuer were momentarily hidden from public eye. No one milled on the street with them this second. The police cars were all just parked for the night.

It was time for the sneak to make his move. He scurried up beside his victim. Just as his prey heard him and turned his head, in the blink of an eye, his attacker wielded a large carving knife.

The Savage Pride cowboy never knew what hit him. He caught a flash as a solitary street light shone in the shiny knife blade. Then that same blade slashed across his throat, opening a cavernous hole as it peeled protective flesh back like tissue paper.

His attacker pushed the knife deeper, hitting bone and severing vocal cords, so his victim could only flail his arms about and make perverse popping and grunting sounds. Warm fluid gushed and poured from the mortal wound, spilling down the front of his chosen victim, onto his assailant's leg and shoe to pool on the sidewalk below. A black cowboy hat tumbled from the dying man's head and landed with a soft plop in his own blood.

His attacker wrapped his arm tightly around the man's body and began walking his limp, useless legs farther along the sidewalk. It appeared he might be helping a drunk along the city streets, except for the bloody trail they were leaving. Realizing that he could not drag his victim's deadweight far, the murderer discarded the body at the top of some steps leading under the Gaylord.

Taking a second to catch his breath, the killer reached into his pocket and pulled forth a pair of handcuffs. He quickly snapped one cuff into place on the man's wrist and the other on the stairway rail. Then, as usual, he maneuvered the knife one last time down low on the man's body leaving his calling card. "Bye, Mason," he said with a wicked chuckle. "I've gone and killed a musical icon. What a thrill!" he proclaimed with glee, slipping off into the darkness.

* * * *

Security guard Bart Melton decided to go back to the Gaylord, in hopes his charge had headed back there. The Nashville strip had been nuts – people everywhere. Bart had lost his assignee in the crowd. One minute he had his eye on the guy, and the next, it was like he had vanished into thin air. Bart had searched the club they were in – bathrooms and all – and looked around on the street, as best he could through all the people. But there had been no sight of his charge. So the only other thing he could think to do was to return to the Gaylord.

As he turned the corner, however, something on the sidewalk immediately demanded his attention. Bart stopped in his tracks, pulled a small flashlight from his belt, and turned it on. With his heart beating in his mouth, Bart shined his flashlight on a large, dark red puddle. There was a cowboy hat amidst it.

As Bart shined his flashlight around, further investigating, he could see more of the substance splattered along the sidewalk and two sets of footprints leading toward a stairwell going under the building. "Crap!" he swore. "I gotta get the police," Bart spoke aloud, rocking back and forth and feeling sick to his stomach. "Christ, I hope that cowboy hat doesn't belong to anyone I know," he mumbled, turning and racing back toward the front of the building and the entrance to the police substation.

* * * *

Surprised to find Callie outside of the bus in the dock area, he glanced about. No one was watching. Callie appeared to be all alone. She knew better than to step forth from the bus without security. He needed to teach her a lesson. He could not withstand the sweet temptation.

He quietly sneaked up behind her and grabbed her from behind. He was not prepared for the bloodcurdling scream that echoed off all the concrete walls surrounding them. His ears were still ringing when she threw a fierce elbow to his ribcage. His arms sprang open, and he dropped what he had in his hand. As he staggered backwards, grimacing in pain and fighting to take a breath, something tumbled from his body, landing behind his back.

Before he could reposition himself, Callie twirled around and landed a kick down low. When he bent downward, she leaped on top of him, grabbing his shirt and hoisting it over his head. He buckled to his knees, as she began pounding him in the head with her fists.

"What's going on over there?!" Callie heard someone shout.

She looked up to see a male security guard. He lit her and her attacker up with a handheld flashlight.

"This man attacked me," Callie screamed, releasing his shirt and stumbling away from him.

"What's the deal here, buddy?" the security guard asked, approaching the individual doubled over on the pavement.

As the person slowly disengaged from the shirt tangled around their head and hands, the security guard's light revealed the identity of the attacker. "What the...?" he asked, shocked to see who it was.

"My God!" Callie exclaimed in shock.

As the security guard helped Callie's victim to his feet, Debbie Gray called to them all. "What's up?"

Callie briefly turned her head to give Debbie a glance. Then she focused her attention back on the gentleman at the male security guard's side. As the security guard helped to stabilize him, Mason stood rubbing his head and side. He quickly explained to them all, "I was just trying to teach Callie a lesson about being out by herself...."

"Looks like you're the one who got taught a lesson...a lesson in what happens to anyone who sneaks up on me," Callie told him, sounding irate, but she scrambled over to her husband's side. She heard something crunch and looked down to see that she had stepped on and crushed Mason's glasses. She figured he must have dropped them in the struggle. "Are you alright?" she asked with concern.

"I think I'll live," he answered, still trying to catch his breath. He hurt from head to toe.

"Where's your security guy?" the guard in uniform asked.

"My security guard went inside to clock out. I'm sure he's gone by now. He figured he was done for the night, since I'm back safe and sound at the bus. Or...was supposed to be."

Before either of the security guards could say more, Bart Melton appeared with two police officers in tow. "Clark, Debbie, these guys need to talk to us outside," Bart told the other security guards. "We have a situation," he said, talking more to Clark and Debbie than Mason and Callie.

"What's going on?" Debbie asked a second time.

"It doesn't involve Robert, does it?" Mason asked with concern, recognizing Bart as Robert's security guard.

"We...uh...we just need to go and talk to the police, and let them do their jobs. I'd like for you and your wife to step inside your motor coach." Bart evasively replied. His eyes looked troubled. "Debbie, will you see they get back to their bus? Then you can join us outside," he strongly suggested.

"Alright," Debbie agreed. "Come on, guys," she said to Mason and Callie. "I'll walk you to your bus."

"Okay," Mason reluctantly agreed. He had a bad feeling about the police being there and Robert's security guard being with them – without Robert. Mason wondered if Robert had gotten himself into some kind of trouble. He hoped not.

Mason turned and stooped down, picking up the cowboy hat that had fallen in back of him in the struggle. Standing, he swiveled back around, and placed his arm around Callie. Leading her toward their bus, the question suddenly dawned on him, "Who's watching Sarah?"

"Debbie Gray *was*," Callie replied, sounding a little perturbed. "She has a little girl around the same age," Callie explained. "I was just taking a little breather. Walking around outside the bus a little. I didn't expect to be scared half out of my wits, or to have security guards rushing over."

"I'm sorry," Mason said to both Callie and Debbie, looking sheepish.

"It's okay," Debbie told him. "I was coming to get Callie anyway. Sarah is back asleep now, but she woke up sick to her stomach. I kind of caught the brunt of her attack. My uniform and shoes were saturated. Needless to say, I had to change clothes."

As she said this, Callie noticed for the first time that Debbie was no longer in uniform. "I'm sorry about Sarah throwing up on you," she said.

"Don't worry about it," Debbie said with a smile. "Like I told you, I have a daughter about the same age. My uniform will wash and so will my shoes. I think Sarah will be fine," she assured Callie. "I don't even think she's running a fever. I'd say something she ate just upset her stomach."

"I don't know. She was really fussy this evening. Maybe she has a virus," Callie said. "Anyway…thanks for watching her."

"No problem," Debbie said, as they all approached the motor coach. "You guys go inside with your daughter, and I'll go and see if I can find out what's going on outside this private parking area," she told them.

"I'd appreciate that," Mason told her.

"Thanks again, Debbie," Callie said as she and Mason rushed aboard the bus to check on their daughter.

Debbie hurried off. She had bagged up her uniform, socks and shoes in a trash bag and stuck it in her locker. She wanted to get this bag out as quickly as possible. She would take it out and put it in the trunk of her car. Then she would discard of it later. She was not going to try and wash these. She had other uniform clothes and shoes.

On a mission, Debbie rushed toward the entertainment center. Once she cleaned out her locker, she would check out the action on the side of the building.

Chapter 7

Restless Night

8:00 a.m. – a screaming alarm clock demanded Wally's attention. A deliberate slap of his hand silenced it. Rolling onto his back, Wally blinked at the muted sun rays that shone through his window shade across the room. Stretching, he was surprised to find he was still very tired.

That's strange. I went to bed early the night before. It's probably a side effect from the painkillers I took, he concluded, automatically reaching to rub his forehead. Wally had suffered another killer headache last evening. The headaches were getting more frequent. *I really do need to make an appointment with a neurologist*, he told himself.

Sitting up on the side of the bed, Wally discovered his right arm was sore. It almost felt as if he had strained a muscle. *It's not my left arm, so it's probably not heart related*, he diagnosed with some relief.

When Wally stood, he noted that his right leg was also a bit stiff. *Damn migraines! They make you sore all over*, he cursed his symptoms.

Rubbing his arm and favoring his left leg, Wally ambled out of the bedroom and into his bathroom. In the bathroom, he was surprised to find the shower doors open and his bath towel missing. Only a hand towel hung haphazardly on the rack. He reached to straighten it, and he slid the shower doors closed. He did not like things to be out of place or order.

I don't remember taking a shower last night, but I guess I did, he concluded, rubbing his head again. Walking over to the toilet, Wally found the toilet seat already raised. *I must have really been out of it last night*, he mused with frustration.

Even though Wally lived alone – a confirmed bachelor – he never left his toilet seat up. As a child, his mother had drummed into his head that it must be kept down. So, usually, not only did he lower the toilet seat after he urinated, but he usually lowered the lid as well. Wally kept a tidy house.

As he reached to untie his sleep pants, he noticed his nails. They had been clipped almost to the quick. Wally also noted his hands were red and tender. *Was I scrubbing my hands?* he wondered in trepidation, as he emptied his bladder.

Flushing the toilet and putting the toilet seat and lid down, he swiveled and sat. Dropping his bald head into his hands, Wally rubbed his eyes. *I've got to get these damn migraines under control*, he told himself. *My memory lapses are getting worse.* He could not allow these things to interfere with his life. *I'll make an appointment with a neurologist today. They can run an MRI or CT and rule out me having a brain tumor or something*, he pondered.

He had his life back together now. Wally could not let some crazy headaches get in his way. After all, he had not let the ugliness from Bowling Green destroy him – not that it had been his fault. A woman Wally was treating had committed suicide and decided to take her husband and two daughters out at the same time.

To spare the hospital any embarrassment, Wally had resigned his position as Chief Psychiatric Counsel at the *Greenview Medical Center*. Still hounded by reporters and chastised by members of the girl's family, he had decided to make a clean break not only with the hospital, but with Bowling Green, Kentucky as well.

It had been hard for a man past middle age – fifty one – to start all over again, but Wally had managed to do so. His private practice was steadily growing. Unfortunately, the added stress had caused Wally to start having migraines, and along with the migraines came memory lapses from time to time.

Wally could handle an occasional throbbing headache. After all, he had suffered from these his entire life. He could also handle sporadic, temporary memory loss. He had also experienced these spells on and off most of his life.

But now, these headaches and odd spells were starting to interfere with his life. He needed to remember therapy sessions, and he needed to remember what he did in his own home. Wally had several neurologist friends. Making an appointment with one could only work to his advantage. If nothing else, they could probably prescribe some wonder drug to keep his migraines under control.

Wally got up from the toilet. Washing his hands, he vacated the bathroom and headed back to his bedroom to get dressed. He had a patient coming to his office at 9:00 a.m., and he did not want to be late. He would call Dr. Jackson Lipton, a neurologist friend, today, and set up an appointment. *Everything will be okay*, he convinced himself. *A few headaches aren't going to hold me back.*

With this resolve firmly in mind, Wally got his normal day underway, going over to his closet to pick out a suit, shirt and tie to wear.

Chapter 8

Disclosure

Scott stood in front of an unobstructed window in an empty apartment unit. He aimed his small camcorder, zooming in, toward the backyard of a residential home across the street from him. On the third floor in the apartment complex, his view of this backyard was perfect. On ground level, a tall privacy fence would have blocked his view.

Scott had just laid a pair of binoculars down on the floor after spotting the man he had been looking for. Now, he switched on his camcorder and began to film proof that this man, while permanently disabled, was still able to build a deck in back of his home. Scott was working an insurance fraud case. Once he got this film back to the company that had hired him, it would mean big bucks for Scott and a loss of benefits for the man across the way.

Scott had crept around the residential home across the street for over a week. He knew the man he was investigating was working on building something in the back of his house. Scott could hear the sound of hammering and other tools being used. But because of the house's high privacy fence, with little-to-no space between the boards, he could not capture the proof he needed.

Scott smiled as the camera buzzed, capturing indisputable images of this man's fraud. He would owe some of his salary to the landlord of this apartment complex. Scott had lucked into there being an empty unit right across from the man he needed to track. He had agreed to pay the landlord a month and a half's rent for the use of this unit, even though he assured the man he would be done in less than a week. This was only his third day in the apartment.

I love it when a plan comes together, Scott relished, as he heard his cell phone ring.

He carefully placed the camcorder on a tripod, glancing into the viewer to make sure he still had a perfect shot. Then he reached into the pocket of his jeans and extracted his cell phone. Taking his eye away from the camcorder, he looked down at his cell phone. His caller ID alerted him that this was a call he should take.

Opening his phone, Scott placed it up to his ear. "Hello." He bent and put his eye to the camcorder as he waited for a response.

"Is this Scott Arnold?" Sherri Ball asked. Scott recognized her accent. It warmed his heart.

"Yes, it is," he answered. "What's up, Detective Ball? Do you have some more information for me about the Jack Jordan homicide?" Scott wasted no time inquiring. He swiveled the camcorder to keep the man across the street – and his fraudulent activities – clearly in view.

"I do have a bit more information about his murder," Sherri shared. "But actually…I was callin' about another murder that just occurred early this mornin' in Nashvill'."

Scott pulled away from the camcorder and stood up straight, fully giving Sherri his attention now. "I'm listening," he said.

"A member of Savage Pride's band had his throat slit about one-thirty this mornin'. He was found close to the Gaylord Center, handcuffed and with a knife down low. Obviously the MO is the same as Jack Jordan, and your Kentucky victims. You said you thought your perp would kill again, and it appears you were right."

"And it's been less than a month since Jack Jordan's murder," Scott commented.

"Three weeks, to be exact," Sherri clarified.

"I didn't think it would be long before Jeanette killed again," Scott told her. "You said you also had some more info on Jack's homicide. What have you found?"

He took another quick glance through his camcorder lens. He watched his 'paycheck' pick up a heavy pile of lumber and carry it a few feet. He swiveled the camcorder to film this scenario, even though he already had more than enough footage to prove his client's case of fraud. Letting the camera roll, Scott straightened up and completely tuned his ears to what Sherri had to say.

"The mould of the footprint, found at the Jordan murder scene, seems to belong to some sort of uniform shoe. We're still checkin' treads to see if we can narrow down which brands. The shoe size appears to be an eight or eight-and-a-half. Also...the depth of the indention seems to indicate that the killer weighs approximately 175 or 180 pounds. A little heavy for your perp...wouldn't you say?"

"Hmm...," Scott murmured. "Our records showed Jeanette at about 150...or 155. He's very thickset, and carries his weight well though. He could have easily put on weight in the year and a half he's been missing. Maybe on purpose...to change his appearance. Did Roger give you his physical description?"

"Yeah. He e-mailed that to me. I've shared your information, and that from the LMPD, with the MNPD. Until we know different, we are all workin' the same case now," Sherri told him.

"Sherri, I really appreciate you calling and letting me know about the latest murder and what you found at the Jordan homicide. Who are the Nashville investigators assigned to the case?" Scott asked.

"Are you plannin' on going to Nashvill' to pick their brains like you did mine?" she asked.

"Yeah...something like that," Scott admitted with a knowing chuckle. He reached to switch off the video camera. Once he took the film footage to his current employer, this case would be wrapped up. So he would have a little free time to do some investigating on his own in Nashville.

"Are you busy tomorrow mornin'?" Sherri surprised Scott by asking.

"What time?" he asked.

"Say...around ten," she replied. "That's eleven o'clock your time," she further pointed out.

"I can be free then," he told her. "What did you have in mind?"

"Why don't you meet me at the Hendersonvill' PD and I'll give you a ride to Nashvill' PD. Those guys aren't as free to share knowledge with PI's as I was," she explained. "If I go in with you, they might be a little freer with information."

"You know, Sherri? I like you more and more all the time," Scott said, a lilt to his voice. "I'll see you at ten Central, tomorrow. Should I come up to your office?"

"No...no need," she replied. "I'll meet you in the lobby. If I get called away on a case or somethin', I'll call your cell phone to let you know. Okay?"

"A-Okay!" Scott agreed. He was looking forward to seeing Detective Ball again. And once more, he was excited to have yet another lead to finding – and hopefully catching – Jeanette. *I'm going to get you, Jeanette. Thanks for coming out of hiding finally,* Scott contemplated with a rush of euphoria. As he ended his call with Sherri, he clapped his hands and shuffled his feet in a little dance of celebration. *Nashville...here I come!*

Chapter 9

Nashville PD

As promised, Scott met Sherri at 10:00 a.m. CST. Sherri awaited him in the lobby when he arrived. She watched him dash in out of the pouring rain. They were the only two in the lobby other than the information officer, who was situated behind his desk.

Scott stood on the police emblem rug just inside the door and shook like a wet dog. He reached to push several strands of wet black hair out of his eyes. The front of his jeans and his entire leather tennis shoes were well saturated. Only Scott's upper body was relatively dry, protected by his water-pearled nylon jacket.

In contrast, Scott noted Sherri's impeccable appearance – fitted Lennon pantsuit; luminous, wavy brown hair; sensitive brown eyes; full, ruby lips; and straight white teeth. Sherri's welcoming smile warmed him, even though his wet clothes chilled.

Regardless of Scott's disgruntled appearance, his mood did not seem to be hampered. Showing sparkling teeth, he greeted, "Hello, Sherri. How are you this dreary, wet day?"

"I'm fine," she replied. Scott listened intently as Sherri continued to talk. "I bet it was an ugly drive from Louisvill'. I'm glad you made it here safe," she said, her worry seeming very genuine.

Her concern warmed Scott's heart a bit more. "The drive was a piece of cake," he downplayed. It had been an *ugly* drive – accidents, fog and low visibility. If he had not left his house early, he would have been late to meet Sherri.

"Well...are you ready to brave the rain again? Or would you like to get a cup of coffee and dry out a little?" Sherri offered, showing true southern hospitality.

"I'm fine," Scott assured her. "My only question is...who's driving?"

"I'll drive," Sherri told him. "My car's probably farther from the door than yours. But I own one of these," she said, holding up a small umbrella. "So we'll be just fine. Shall we go?" she asked.

"Sounds good by me," Scott agreed, turning toward the doors.

He was surprised when Sherri linked her arm with his. "Here. You take this umbrella and hold it over both of us. You're a bit taller than me," she pointed out with a grin.

Scott took the umbrella from Sherri's hand. As he pushed open the glass door leading outdoors, he punched the plastic button on the umbrella, sending it open with a swoosh. He held it over both their heads. The close proximity of their bodies allowed Scott to savor the scent of Sherri's perfume once more. He tried to ignore the smell, but it made his head swim and his heart ache.

Scott was glad when they got to Sherri's car, a black Buick LeSabre, and he was able to separate from her. As soon as she was settled inside the car, he put the umbrella down, allowing the cool rain to wash over his face, squelching his desires and washing away sad memories. Opening his car door, he climbed into the car with Sherri. He placed the closed, wet umbrella down beside his soggy tennis shoes and shut the door.

"Man...what a glutton for punishment you are!" Sherri accused, looking at the rain water running down his face and pearling on his jacket. "I give you an umbrella and you put it down early and let yourself get wet. Macho Man syndrome, right?" she teased with a chuckle.

"Something like that," Scott replied in a gruff voice, trying to ignore the fact that he could once again smell her perfume – *so like Debbie's*. He looked out the front window.

"So are we headed out?" he asked, still sounding much too serious.

"Yeah," Sherri answered, the smile leaving her face. Scott's sudden abruptness and the rigidity of his body disturbed her. *Maybe he's just anxious for information on the Nashville murder. More pieces to his puzzle. He wants this murderer caught in the worst way. And so do we. We'll all make an awesome team.* Without further adeiu, she started the car to head out.

* * * *

Sherri drove them to the James Robertson Parkway where the Metropolitan Nashville Police Department is located. Sherri and Scott did not engage in a lot of conversation during the drive there. Other sounds filled the void: The windshield wipers swiping back and forth in erratic movement; the police radio buzzing as the dispatcher called out codes and locations of crimes; the humming defroster; and the LeSabre's tires sloshing through water standing on the roadways. The heat inside the car, for the most part, dried Scott's wet hair and clothing.

He was relieved when they arrived at the police station: a large, brick, L-shaped, three-story building with an eye-pleasing brick spiral in front. Once inside the building, they headed to the glassed-in information booth directly ahead of them. A security guard in the booth called homicide detective Lieutenant Geoff Gregory for them.

A few moments later, the lieutenant opened the door to the left of the information booth and ushered Sherri and Scott inside. The lieutenant was dressed professionally in a black, pinstriped suit. In his late forties, Geoff was a seasoned investigator of many years. Thinning gray hair and lines on his face showed the strain of investigating and solving many murders in Nashville.

"Sherri, it's good to see you again," Geoff greeted with a smile, reaching to squeeze her hand.

Scott noticed that Lieutenant Gregory also gave Sherri's body an obvious appraisal. A moment later, he finally allowed his eyes to settle on Scott. Granting him a quick visual inspection, Lt. Gregory's lips pursed. When his eyes settled back on Scott's face, their harshness relayed the lieutenant's disapproval at Scott's casual disarray.

Looking back at Sherri and smiling again, Geoff suggested, "Sherri, why don't we all go into one of the conference rooms where we can talk privately."

"Sounds good by me," Sherri agreed.

As Geoff – a tall man like Scott – strutted down the hall, Scott easily kept pace. Sherri's much shorter legs struggled to keep up.

The MNPD conference room was much more upscale than the small meeting room in Hendersonville. Padded office chairs surrounded a long, maple table. The floors were carpeted, and alabaster wall sconces provided a dreamy glow to the room.

They all had a seat at the end of the table. Lieutenant Gregory sat in the end chair, like he was king, and Scott and Sherri sat on each side of him across the table from one another. "Geoffrey, this is Investigator Scott Arnold," Sherri enlightened him when they were all seated. "I brought him along to share his knowledge from the LMPD on similar homicides that occurred in Louisvill', Kentucky, about a year-and-a-half ago."

"Nice to meet you, Detective Arnold," Geoff addressed him, giving him an odd look again, but he offered his hand. "I'm Lieutenant Geoff Gregory."

Scott flashed a conspiratorial smile at Sherri before he reached to shake Geoff's hand. He wondered why she had made it sound as if he were still a detective with the LMPD and not just a private investigator. He figured Sherri must have valid reasons for the pretext, so Scott decided to go along with it. "Nice to meet you, Lieutenant Gregory," Scott said.

"So I take it you think your Kentucky killer has moved on to Tennessee," Geoff conjectured.

"Yes, sir," Scott answered, nodding his head. "The MO from some of our cases matches almost identically to the MO in the Hendersonville case. And from what Sherri has told me, this latest homicide in Nashville falls along the same line. We know that our Kentucky killer skipped town, and his trail had gone cold before I learned of the Hendersonville homicide. As I shared with Detective Ball, our killer – a man by the name of Jeanette Peterson…"

"A *man* named *Jeanette?*" Geoff questioned, raising an eyebrow and snickering.

"Yes, Jeanette is a man. From what we could track of his background, he had breast augmentation done as a teenager. So Jeanette looks like a woman, but his DNA proves he is one hundred percent *male*. And his DNA also links him to the scene of two of our murders. He has a direct link to two other gruesome homicides as well. We consider this man to be very devious and dangerous. A sociopath who longs to kill and thirsts for blood. If he isn't caught, he will continue to kill," Scott said with conviction, his dark eyes levelly meeting Geoff's gray ones.

"Scott told me the same thing in Hendersonvill'," Sherri chimed in. "And now, this murder's taken place in Nashvill'. I believe we have a serial killer on our hands, and I believe it may be the same serial killer they are seekin' in Kentucky."

"That well could be," Geoff agreed, swiveling his chair and tapping the ends of his fingers together. "But, regardless, I'm a little surprised to see you here in Nashville, Detective Arnold. Why didn't you just call and share what information the LMPD has? Needless to say, you are out of your jurisdiction. This is for MNPD homicide to investigate. Naturally, we'll be more than happy to let the LMPD know when we've caught our killer. And then, if it's the same person, I'm sure the LMPD will have him…or her…extradited back to Kentucky to stand trial for the crimes this person committed there. But we have a very competent homicide squad here in Nashville, Detective Arnold. We really don't need your manpower to help. Is that understood?"

"Perfectly," Scott confirmed, glancing at Sherri to find her grimacing. "I didn't come here to try and take over your case, Lieutenant. I have a personal stake in tracking down this particular killer. He...he killed...my...my fiancé...or at least she would have been my fiancé. I had...actually still have...the ring, but I never got a chance to give it to her," Scott confessed, looking down at the table for a moment.

Hearing Scott's words and seeing his face contort with pain, Sherri's heart twisted once more. She watched and listened as Scott reined in his emotions, looked Geoff back in the eye, and continued, "This killer needs to be caught so he can't go on killing innocent people and destroying loved ones' lives. I just want to share knowledge and see if I can help your detectives find him as soon as possible."

"I can appreciate that, Detective Arnold," Geoff said. Lowering his eyes and clearing his throat, he added, "I'm sorry about your loss." Making eye contact again, he agreed, "We do need to find this killer as soon as possible and keep him...or her...from destroying any more lives. But MNPD needs to handle the investigation. I would rather you go back to Louisville and await our call. I'm sure you are a fine investigator, but we don't need you snooping around here. You'll only be in the way, and you'll slow us down."

"So does that mean you don't intend to share any of the details of this new homicide with me?" Scott asked, giving him an unyielding glare and pursing his lips.

"I see no merit in doing so," Geoff answered, leaning back in his chair and folding his hands over his heart. "We'd love for you to go back to Louisville and have the LMPD send us whatever profiling, physical description, and MO's your department would like to share. And, as I said, if we find that our killer ties in with yours, then we will let the LMPD know as soon as we apprehend our killer. You don't have a place here, Detective Arnold. We can't have you going on a personal vendetta in Nashville."

"That's not my intention," Scott argued, gritting his teeth. He rolled back his chair and stood. "There's no sense me wasting my time here," he said, balling his fists. His eyes also blazed.

Sherri also rolled back her chair and stood. She threw her purse strap over her shoulder. "Scott, why don't I walk you out?" she offered. Then, laying a hand on Geoff's shoulder, she asked, "Geoffrey, can you and I have a word in private in a sec?"

"Of course we can, Sherri," he agreed with a smile. Looking over at Scott, he said, "Detective Arnold, thank you for coming to Nashville. I'll be awaiting a call from the LMPD."

"A detective by the name of Roger Matthews will be calling you," Scott told him. "He's the detective assigned to the case now."

"Roger Matthews," Geoff repeated. "I look forward to his call."

"You do that," Scott snapped with an ugly curl to his lip.

He turned and propelled his legs behind the Lieutenant's chair. Grasping the brass door handle and jerking it downward, the door released with a click and Scott pulled it open. Stepping outside, he waited for Sherri to also vacate the room. She quietly shut the door behind her.

Motioning for Scott to follow her up the hall, Sherri turned and began making her way toward the exit. As they walked the hallway, they passed several others, some coming out of offices. At the end of the hall, by the exit door leading into the lobby, two padded, vinyl chairs sat by the wall, with a picture of downtown Nashville perfectly situated between them.

Sherri took a seat in one of the chairs, tossing her purse on the floor beside it. She pointed to the other chair, attempting to get Scott to sit also. He walked over and leaned against a side wall instead, placing one of his feet up on the baseboard, and aimlessly watching others as they walked the hallway, ducked into offices spaces, and came and went through the exit door.

"Well, that was a huge waste of time," he said, still sounding angry. "Lieutenant Gregory is a real pain in the ass, isn't he?" he snarled. He kept his voice low because he realized that some of the other people in the hall might well know the lieutenant.

"He can be...yes," Sherri admitted, nodding her head. "Look...he has no reason not to share information with me, Scott. Our two departments will be workin' hand-in-hand to solve these murders. I'm goin' to go back and talk with him. I'll let you know what I find out. Okay?"

"You'd do that?" Scott asked with surprise, placing both feet flat on the ground and meeting her eyes.

"Of course I would, Scott," she said, her eyes conveying her support. "I'm not as hard-nosed as Lieutenant Gregory. I believe all law enforcement is on the same team, regardless of jurisdiction. I want the same thing you do, Scott...this killer caught...and caught ASAP. And I think if we share information with one another, we can accomplish that much quicker than tryin' to re-create the wheel. Now...will you please have a seat and wait for me? I want to get back before Geoffrey changes his mind about talkin' to me."

Scott watched as Sherri stood. She pointed to one of the chairs. Like an obedient child, he took a step, turned and sat down. Sherri pushed her purse over beside Scott's chair. "Watch my purse for me, will you?" she asked, half demanding.

Not waiting for Scott's reply, she started down the hall. Scott watched as Sherri weaved through people, making her way back toward the conference room. She did not even give him another glance.

Scott could not help but feel grateful to Sherri for what she was doing. She seemed to want to work with him to find the killer. Scott liked Detective Sherri Ball a great deal. He also noted, as he watched her shapely hips sway, that she was not a hard woman to look at either.

Keep your mind focused, he chastised himself. *I need to track down Jeanette. That's what's most important. Everything else comes second.* Scott glanced at his watch, and he waited, hoping Sherri had some luck getting the facts in this latest murder investigation. If she did not, he would do some private investigating on his own. He would track down the information he needed…with or without the help of the MNPD.

Chapter 10

The Breakfast

Twenty minutes later, Scott finally saw Sherri and Lieutenant Gregory making their way up the hall toward him. "Sherri, as always, it's been a pleasure," Scott heard Geoff say to her. Geoff also gave her a smile and squeezed a hand. Sherri's other hand held her closed umbrella.

As the lieutenant turned to make his way through a door leading to his office, he gave Scott a nod, dismissing him. Scott merely gave Geoff an aggravated stare in response. Scott watched this man disappear behind a door. Then he stood as Sherri approached him.

"Ready for me to give you a ride back to your car?" Sherri asked.

"Sure," Scott replied, trying to read her eyes. Curiosity was killing him to find out if Sherri had been able to get any details out of the lieutenant, or if he had blown her off too.

Sherry bent to scoop up her purse and throw its strap over her shoulder. Scott walked two steps and open the exit door leading into the lobby.

Thunder rumbled and lightening flashed as they approached the front doors. "Yuck! Now it's stormin'," Sherri commented, stopping and standing amidst some uniformed cops and a few civilians.

They all seemed to be waiting out the storm before going outside. The lobby had brown tile and brick walls, so it was already dark. The stormy weather made it outright gloomy, but the outside scenario was worse. Wind whipped large raindrops in circles; umbrellas flipped inside out as pedestrians fought with them and lost; city litter swirled in the air.

"I don't want to drive in this mess," Sherri revealed, glancing at Scott.

One of the female police officers decided to be helpful to the visitors. She told everyone that was standing and watching the storm, "Folks, there's a cafeteria on the second floor if any of you want to sit down, drink a cup of coffee, maybe grab a snack and wait 'til this passes over."

"What do you say?" Sherri asked Scott, jumping as a loud clap of thunder shook the building.

"Can we talk there?" Scott asked. He would brave the storm and drive Sherri's car if that's what it took to find out if she had discovered anything from Lieutenant Gregory.

"I don't see why we couldn't," Sherri replied.

"Then lead the way," Scott said.

Sherri turned and began making her way through the horde of people. Scott followed close at her heels. A moment later, they were aboard an elevator car and stepping off onto the second floor.

They followed others down the hall toward the small cafeteria. But they could have just as easily followed their noses. Delectable aromas called to them: bacon frying and coffee percolating. Walking into the bright cafeteria – several fluorescent lights in a white-tiled ceiling, white stucco walls, and gleaming, black-and-white speckled, granite tile – Scott, Sherri and those in front of them all headed toward the food-serving line. Scott grabbed a plastic tray and placed it on the iron bar railing in front of him.

"Are you goin' to eat?" Sherri asked him.

"That bacon smells too good to pass up," Scott answered, salivating. He slid his tray forward as the line in front of him inched along. "I've had stale donuts and coffee this morning, and that's it," he admitted.

"Well, I've had breakfast, so I'll just get some coffee," Sherri told him.

She reached to extract a white coffee mug from a rack beside Scott's head. Stepping over to the coffee dispenser across the way, she filled her cup with the fresh steamy brew. She mixed in sugar and creamer and headed for the cashier at the end of the line.

An older lady, with gray hair in a net, told Sherri, "That'll be a dollar-seventy-five."

Sherri sat her steaming cup and her umbrella on the counter in front of this woman. She pulled her purse from her shoulder, sat it on the railing, fished out her wallet, and pulled forth two one-dollar bills, handing them to this woman. The cash register dinged and the drawer popped opened. The cashier scratched through some coins, extracting two dimes and a nickel. She placed these coins into the palm of Sherri's hand.

"Thank you," Sherri said.

The woman merely nodded.

Sherri dropped the coins in her change purse, slid her wallet back into her purse, and slung the bag over her shoulder. Picking up her coffee and umbrella, she headed toward a small vacant table in the corner of the dining room, away from the windows. The tables and chairs were filling up fast.

Lightening zigzagged repeatedly in the sky outside, flashing like a strobe light within the cafeteria. Thunder shook the building again and again, and rain streamed down the windows as if someone was hitting them with a spray nozzle.

Sherri sat down and waited for Scott to join her. A few moments later, Scott pulled out the chair across from Sherri and sat. He placed his orange tray on the table in front of him. A plentiful heaping of scrambled eggs, bacon, and hash browns encompassed a white Styrofoam plate. Scott also had a steaming cup of black coffee.

He reached to grab both the plastic salt and pepper shakers. Seeing Sherri looking at him, Scott paused before doctoring any of his food with the spices. "Are you sure you don't want anything?" he asked. "I'm sure I could get another plate, and we could split my breakfast. I've got plenty."

"No," she declined. "I'm fine with just coffee. You enjoy your breakfast."

"That I will," Scott agreed, liberally salting and peppering his eggs and hash browns. Picking up a plastic fork, he dug in, taking first a bite of scrambled eggs, then some hash browns, and lastly, a bite of bacon. He hardly seemed to chew before he washed down his first sampling with some coffee.

Sherri smiled and commented, "You eat like a starvin' person."

"Oh…sorry," Scott apologized, chewing up what he had left in his mouth, wiping his mouth with a napkin, and putting his fork down for a moment. "I'm not much of a cook, so when I get good cooking, I tend to scarf it down…even when it's at a police headquarters' cafeteria."

Sherri felt sorry for Scott. *He's a nice-looking man. He should have a woman filling his belly with plenty of home cooking*, she found herself contemplating.

"Anyway…" Scott said, taking another drink of coffee. "Enough about my eating habits. What I need to hear from you is if the dear lieutenant shared any details of his investigation."

"Of course he did," Sherri shared. A huge smile appeared on her face, and her deep chocolate eyes sparkled.

"What did you do…turn on your southern charm?" Scott inquired, taking another bite of scrambled eggs.

"He's southern too, remember?" she replied. "So that wouldn't work…"

"Ah…*contraire*…" Scott argued with a chuckle. "Maybe what I should have asked is if you used your feminine wiles?"

"I'll never tell," Sherri answered, fluttering her eyelashes and giggling.

"You little vixen," Scott teased, savoring another slice of bacon. "So are you going to share these details with me?"

"Hmm...what do I get if I do?" Sherri bantered back, holding her coffee cup between her hands and taking another sip.

"You name it," Scott promised, mixing catsup with his hash browns and taking another bite. He finished chewing his food, and wiped his mouth before suggesting, "Dinner?"

"Would that be dinner alone...or dinner with you?" Sherri asked.

"Whichever you prefer," Scott was quick to agree.

"You're too easy. Almost a pushover," Sherri mocked with a toothy grin, taking another sip of coffee. "Okay... dinner it is," she agreed, sitting her cup back on the table. "I'll have to think on whether I want dinner alone...or with you," she snickered, continuing their repartee.

"Whatever the lady wants," Scott agreed again, filling his mouth with more eggs. "Now...spill!" he ordered, arching his fingers upward and moving them toward him.

"Okay...okay," she agreed, surrendering. Lowering her voice an octave, so as not to be overheard by the tables around them, she leaned closer to Scott and began, "The killer left bloody footprints. The shoes had heavy tread on the bottom...just like the shoes worn by our killer in Hendersonvill'. Again, they appear to be uniform shoes..."

"So were the security guards questioned?" Scott asked. "And...were any of the guards female?"

"Yes...and yes," Sherri answered. "The security guard that notified the police was not in uniform. He had been assigned to bodyguard the victim, so he went into town with him in plain clothes. Once in town, he lost the victim in the crowd. Evidently, the victim had been headed back to the Gaylord...but he was murdered before he made it," she relayed, pausing to drink more of her coffee. Sitting the cup back on the table, she continued, "The other male security guard was in uniform. He was questioned and an imprint was taken of the bottom of one of his work shoes. The tread from his shoe had a different pattern than the one left by the killer. The other security guard was…you guessed it…a woman…"

"And was she questioned as well?" Scott was anxious to know.

He had pushed his tray aside, even though he still had some eggs, one slice of bacon, and some hash browns left. His focus was no longer on food. His focus was totally on what Sherri had to say now. Because Sherri had lowered her voice, he had been fighting to hear her. But now, his ears were so attuned to her words that it seemed the whole rest of the cafeteria had gone mute, even though all of the conversations going on around them caused a dim roar in the room.

"Yes, the female security guard was questioned as well," Sherri answered. "She was not in uniform either. She claimed she had been guardin' Mason Greathouse. The police asked if she had any uniforms on site. She said she did, in a locker inside the buildin'. She voluntarily gave MNPD one of her uniform shoes from her locker. The tread from this shoe did not match either."

"So have the security guards officially been cleared as suspects in this case?" Scott asked, breaking off another piece of bacon and placing it in his mouth. He washed it down with the last of his coffee.

"No one's been cleared as a suspect yet, Scott," Sherri answered, finishing off her own coffee and sitting her empty cup on Scott's tray. "They will all likely be questioned more. At this point though, MNPD homicide has no viable leads."

"Did you perchance get the names of the security guards?" Scott asked, standing and picking up his tray.

"No, I didn't," Sherri revealed. "I won't be questionin' them, Scott. MNPD's Central Patrol Precinct – the one right in front of the Gaylord – will be handlin' the investigation. Homicide investigations in Nashvill' are handled at the precinct where the murder ocurred. Geoffrey promised to enlighten me on any breakthroughs they have in the case though."

"Yeah, I bet," Scott said in a voice laced with cynicism, a deep frown on his face.

"He will share information with me, Scott," Sherri tried to assure him.

Yeah...as little as possible, Scott thought to himself. "Well...I guess that's that," he commented. Then he asked, "So are you about ready to hit the road? I could drive if you'd like."

Sherri glanced toward the windows. The lightening did not seem to be streaking the sky as much. The rain had lessened, and the thunder sounded farther away. "I'm ready if you're ready," she told Scott, also standing. She reached down and pulled her purse and umbrella from the floor. Tossing her purse strap over her shoulder, she said, "I think the storm has lessened some. Regardless, I'm perfectly capable of drivin'. I may not like drivin' in this slop, but I can manage."

"I'm sure you can," Scott said, an easy smile coming to his face. *The lady likes to be in control*, he mused. He rather liked Sherri's independent spirit.

Scott headed toward the nearest trash receptacle. Coffee cups clinked as he removed them from the tray and placed them amongst other dirty cups in a gray, plastic, busboy pan sitting atop one of the trash cans. He spied red lipstick on the rim of Sherri's cup.

The wooden door on a trash bin squeaked as Scott pushed it open and cleared the tray. His plastic tray clattered as he sat it atop other trays on top of the trash receptacle. As Scott turned, he found a woman standing behind him waiting to empty her tray. "Excuse me," he said as he stepped around her.

Looking across the room, he spied Sherri waiting for him in the archway leading out into the hall. He quickly propelled his legs in her direction, passing others at tables and on foot. As he and Sherri vacated the cafeteria, Scott was already mulling over his next plan of action. He was going to track down the names of the security guards on duty the night of the murder, and he was going to find out more about each one of them – especially the female officer. His gut told him he was getting closer to finding Jeanette, and his gut was not often wrong.

Chapter 11

Session Three

The murder of Robert Oaks, keyboardist for Savage Pride, correlated almost perfectly with Debbie's next appointment with Dr. Cleaver. As usual, he was seated behind his desk when Debbie walked in. "Hello, Debbie," he greeted, putting down a pen he had been writing with.

The second day of rain, outdoor Nashville was wet and gloomy. This lack of sunshine was made more evident by Wally's mini-blinds being opened – no sunlight today to hurt his eyes or give him headaches.

"Hello, Wally," Debbie answered, walking over to a coat rack by the couch.

Debbie took off a large, nylon, *Cincinnati Reds* jacket. She placed it on a hanger, and hung it on the rack. She dropped her hand-held umbrella, with a clunk, into a slot at the bottom. Then she turned to face Dr. Cleaver.

Wally noticed that Debbie was in her work uniform again, but he also noted her shoes were different. Instead of her uniform shoes, she wore black leather tennis shoes. Wally found this strange.

Debbie noticed Dr. Cleaver staring at her feet with an odd expression on his face. "I didn't have any uniform shoes to put on today," she explained, wiggling her toes. "One pair is dirty and the police have the other," she further elaborated, meandering over to the chair in front of Dr. Cleaver's desk. She watched Wally's eyes to see how he reacted to this new information.

"Okay," he replied, looking unruffled and rather disinterested. "Did you come here today to talk about your wardrobe?" he challenged.

"Yeah. I'm just here for a social visit. Why do we always have to play these moronic games?" she spewed, rolling her eyes. "You know I'm here to talk about more important things than my shoes, Wally."

"Then why don't you do that?" he solicited, steepling his fingers in front of him. He looked perfectly relaxed. He was used to spells of hostility from Debbie, and he was used to her playing games. In fact, he expected – perhaps even welcomed – these behaviors. Her spurts of anger and game playing were part of her therapy.

Releasing the back of the chair, Debbie strolled over to the window. She grabbed a string and hoisted the mini-blinds up. They made a zipping noise as they rose. Looking out at the pouring rain, Debbie said, in a haunted voice, "This rain is washing blood down into our sewers. Did you know that, Wally?"

"Whose blood, Debbie?" Wally mustered the courage to ask.

"Did you hear about the death of Robert Oaks, Savage Pride's keyboard player?" she asked, turning to face him again. There was a bit of a smirk on her face.

"Of course I did," Wally replied. "You'd have to be in a cave or dead not to have heard about his murder. It's been all over the news…on the TV…in the newspaper…on the internet. What does his death have to do with your turmoil, Debbie?"

"Did you enjoy their concert the other night?" Debbie asked, changing the subject.

"Did *I*?" Wally questioned, looking puzzled. "Savage Pride is a bit too modern of a band for me. I'm more into oldies music…"

"So…why did you come to their concert then?" Debbie asked. "Was it just because I sent you free, choice seat tickets?"

"*Me*? Did you see *me* at their concert?" Wally asked, seeming a little rattled.

"You know I did. I waved at you, and you waved back," Debbie told him. She walked back over to his desk and took a seat. "That was only two nights ago, Wally. Why are you acting like you've forgotten?"

"I…I wasn't feeling well that night," he truthfully relayed, biting the end of his index finger.

"You could have fooled me. You stood the whole concert, clapping and whistling," she relayed, eyeballing him strangely.

"Okay…" he responded, his eyes darting from side to side as he processed this information. *Maybe Debbie saw someone that looked like me. It couldn't have been me. I had a migraine. I took pills for it and went to bed.* "I don't think you came here today to talk about my behavior at a concert either," he addressed her again, sounding aggravated. "You mentioned the keyboard player's murder. Why don't you elaborate on your feelings about that?"

"You want me to elaborate, Wally?" Debbie repeated, her eyes piercing his. "Okay, fine. I'll elaborate. I was there when Robert Oaks died."

"Is that so?" Wally asked, steepling his fingers and leaning back in his chair. He was back in psychiatric mode now. "And I surmise by that statement, I'm supposed to conclude that you killed him as well. You slashed the man's throat, mutilated his body, handcuffed him, and left him to die in some stairwell. Right?"

"You say that almost in jest, Wally," Debbie pointed out, leaning forward in her chair. Grabbing the edge of his desk, her eyes darkened and she warned in a hiss, "I'd advise you not to underestimate me."

"I would never do that, Debbie," he assured her, placing his hands on the arms of his chair. "I think we all have the capacity within us to kill. It's whether we act on these wayward desires and fantasies...or not...that separates those who kill from those who don't. You have to decide which side of the fence you are on. And I think you've chosen to fight these desires and fantasies. That's why you keep coming to see me. Am I wrong?"

"What if I tell you that you *are* wrong?" Debbie taunted him, a crooked smile on her face.

"If you are trying to elude that you *have* crossed the line and become a killer...that you *did*...in fact...kill Robert Oaks, then I'd say you should be sitting down with...and talking with...MNPD homicide and not me," Wally said, a hint of irritation in his voice. He reached and picked up his pen and began rolling it in his hands. "So have our sessions come to an end, Debbie? Do I need to call MNPD homicide and set you up an appointment with them?" he asked, reaching to finger his telephone.

"Whoa...take it easy, Wally," she requested, the smile disappearing from her face. Debbie released his desk and sat back in her chair.

"If you want me to take it easy, then you will *stop* playing games," he told her, shaking his pen at her and taking his hand away from the phone. He also leaned back in his chair.

"Okay," Debbie surrendered. "It's just that Robert Oaks' death...like Jack Jordan's...has me itching to...as you put it...jump on the other side of that fence." *Again*, she thought, but naturally kept to herself. She fully believed Wally would turn her into the authorities if he had any idea how dangerous she really was. "The desires are strong, Wally," she continued, folding her hands and tapping her index fingers to her lips. "I think of Susanna's welfare, and I fight these desires, but it gets harder and harder. Especially with these murders all around me..."

"This last one really hits close to home, doesn't it?" he asked, pulling on his mustache. "I take it you were still working security for Savage Pride when Robert Oaks met his demise. That's what you meant when you said you were there when he died, isn't it?" he asked, sitting back and steepling his fingers in front of him again.

"What else could I have meant?" she replied, answering a question with a question again. "So how do I make these nagging, evil desires to kill stop, Wally?" she fired another question at him, sounding desperate. She also kneaded her hands in her lap.

"Direct the anger at the people it should be directed at, Debbie," the doctor instructed. "The people it should have been directed at all along...your parents."

"My parents are both dead, Wally. Hopefully rotting in hell!" she blurted out with ire, her eyes blazing and her mouth a taut line. *Just like the hell they caused my life to be!*

"But your anger at them is still very much alive, Debbie," he pointed out, picking up his pen and shaking it at her. "In fact, it festers within you like a huge infected sore. The puss oozes out as a desire to hurt others...even kill others. You must heal this sore within you."

"Psycho mumbo jumbo!" Debbie spat. Pushing her robust body out of the chair, she bounced to her feet and began to pace. "That tells me nothing, Wally! What do you want me to do...dig up my parents' skeletons and smash them to smithereens with a sledgehammer. Do you think that would release all of the anger and heal that big, open sore inside of me?!" She almost smiled as she realized that this idea actually appealed to her.

"No, I don't think digging your parents up and smashing their skeletons would be feasible, Debbie," he replied, sitting up tall in his chair. "But we could do some role-playing if you would like."

"Role-playing? What does that mean?" Debbie asked, stopping her pacing and glaring at him with a pinched frown on her full face.

"I could pretend to be your mom and/or your dad, and you could direct your anger at me. You could say to me what you wished you'd had a chance to say to them. Cuss me out or whatever," he explained, leaning back in his chair and folding his hands in front of him.

"Wally, believe me when I say you don't even *remotely* want me to direct my anger at you. That is…if you want to remain among the living," she warned, squeezing the back of the chair so hard it left impressions.

"You know what, Debbie? I'm willing to take my chances," he told her, maintaining eye contact. There was a confident, fearless expression on his face.

"You want to do this today?" she asked, crossing her arms across her chest.

"No. Not today. We would need an entire session for this. I don't want it rushed. And your time is about up," he informed her as he glanced at his watch. "Why don't you see Marissa and set up another appointment for say…. Let's see…today is Monday. How about this Friday?"

"You don't know what you are getting yourself into, Wally," Debbie said. "I'd suggest you remove all sharp objects from the office…like your letter opener…before we start our next session," she advised, eyeballing the gold handle sticking out of his pencil holder.

"Sound advice, Debbie," he said, reaching to extract it. He opened up his squeaky top desk drawer, tossed the letter opener inside with a clunk, and pushed the drawer back closed. Then he added, "Everything will be fine. You'll see. And I think you'll be amazed to find that a lot of your anger will have dissipated after our next session."

"Either that…or Marissa will be calling the coroner," Debbie said with a half smile. She uncrossed her arms, turned, and walked over to the coat rack, gathering her jacket and umbrella. "See you Friday, Wally," she said, sounding almost eager.

"See you then, Debbie," he replied, waving at her as she opened the door.

As she shut the door behind her, Dr. Cleaver reached to pick up his phone. He was going to call his neurologist friend and set up an appointment ASAP. *Just in case I really was at that concert the other night and can't remember it. I need to get to the bottom of these headaches and memory lapses, and I need to get to the bottom of it now!*

Chapter 12

The Names

Wednesday afternoon, a spit-shined and polished Scott – fresh shaven, cologned, every hair in place, dressed in suit and tie with shiny dress shoes – walked into the *Human Resources Department* at the *Gaylord*. The room, lit by decorative, halogen, track lighting, was bright and inviting, even though it was cloudy outside. Scott walked across the carpeted floor toward a granite countered receptionist's station.

An overweight, blond-from-a-bottle lady – who Scott guessed to be in her early twenties – looked up from her desk, and asked, "May I help you?"

"Well…I hope so," Scott answered, flashing a dazzling smile. He placed his hands on the counter between them and leaned in toward this woman. In a quiet voice, he asked, "If I tell you something in confidence, could I trust you to keep a secret? You look like a lady I could trust. Are you?"

With a puzzled, yet interested, expression, this woman's round face and large body quivered with laughter as she replied, "What secret could you tell me? I don't even know you."

"Oh…" Scott chuckled, raising one of his hands and lightly striking his forehead with the palm. "Where are my manners?" he declared with a furrowed brow. "My name is Scott Arnold. In..vesti..gator Scott Arnold to be exact." He offered his hand as he asked, "And who do I have the pleasure of talking to this afternoon?"

"My name is Adrianna...Adrianna Stewart," she answered with a smile, shaking his hand.

"A lovely name for a lovely young lady," Scott commented, showing his gleaming teeth again. He gave her hand an extra brush as he released it.

"Yeah...right!" she replied, rolling her eyes and sounding doubtful. "So what exactly are you after, Mr... um...Investigator Arnold? Are you a police officer?"

"I'm an investigator," he said again, standing tall and thrusting out his chest, as if to denote pride in his position. "Not a beat cop," he clarified. "And you're very perceptive, Adrianna. I *am* after something. Although getting to talk to such a charming lady this morning is certainly a bonus."

"Uh-huh. Enough with the smoozing," she chuckled, bashfully breaking eye contact. Pulling her skirt down a little over her large thighs, she looked back up at Scott, questioning, "So I'll ask you again, Investigator, how can I help you?"

The telephone rang just as Scott was about to tell her. Adrianna held up her index finger, rolled her chair away from him, and picked up her phone. Scott waited, tyring to be patient, as she talked to an unknown person, filled out a "While You Were Away" form, stuck it in the appropriate named slot on the counter, and hung up the phone.

"Sorry for the interruption," Adrianna apologized, rolling her chair back over to the counter and giving Scott her undivided attention once more.

"No problem," Scott said. Leaning back in toward her, he began explaining, barely above a whisper, "Here's my dilemma, Adrianna. I'm a new investigator in the Nashville area. I need to gather some facts about the security guards who were on duty a few days ago when Robert Oaks was murdered."

"Oh!" Adrianna exclaimed, shuddering. "That gives me the creeps. I can't believe he was killed right outside this building. I want the cops to catch that killer fast. I won't feel safe until they do."

"I'm sure you won't," Scott agreed. Taking the liberty of reaching to pat her nearest chubby hand, he elaborated, "And you can help the police catch this killer by providing me with a few tidbits of information. Do you think you can do that?"

"I don't know," Adrianna said, glancing around the office as if someone else might be listening to their conversation. All the office doors were closed and no one else milled in the corridors. "What exactly do you need to know?"

"I...I just need the names of the security guards who were on duty that night. I hate to admit it...but...I...I misplaced my notepad," he admitted, looking down at the counter in seeming embarrassment. Making eye contact with Adrianna again, Scott further explained, "That notepad contained the names of these individuals. I need to follow up with them and ask a few more questions. But that will be a little hard for me if I don't know who the security guards were. Since I'm new guy on the block, my butt could be in a sling if I don't track down the names again." Scott's eyes added more emphasis to his words as they pled for Adrianna's help.

She was silent for a few minutes, and as her eyes moved from side to side and up and down, Scott could tell she was thinking everything over and carefully considering his request. "I don't want to put you out, Adrianna, or cause you any trouble," Scott finally spoke, breaking the awkward silence. "If you giving me these names is a problem, then I don't want you to do it. I'll just 'fess up to my supervisor about losing them, and we'll go from there."

As Scott began to back away from the counter, Adrianna said, "Wait! I don't think me giving you their names would be any big deal. If I don't, you'll probably get into trouble. Then your superior will be back here asking the same questions anyway. Isn't that about right?"

"More than likely," Scott said, rocking a little on his heel, pretending to be nervous.

Adrianna tore off another page from her "While You Were Away" pad. She turned it over and began writing on the blank backside. "Here you go," she said with a slight smile, holding out the slip of paper toward Scott. "Don't lose this."

Scott took the paper from her outstretched hand. Glancing down, he saw that she had written several names on the back. "Adrianna, you're an angel!" Scott gushed with an ear-to-ear smile, placing the piece of paper in his pocket. He closed the distance between himself and the counter again, reaching over and tapping both Adrianna's cushy upper arms in a mock hug. Adrianna's face colored and she giggled. "It's been a pleasure, young lady," Scott said.

"The pleasure was all mine," she said and snickered again. "You guys just get that killer off the street, okay?"

"Will do!" Scott promised, turning to head toward the door. Before he opened it and escaped into the hall, he turned and said, "Thanks again, Adrianna. I'll be seeing you around."

She merely nodded. However, she was thinking to herself, *Don't I wish*. It was not often that Adrianna garnered the attention of a tall, good-looking, great-smelling guy like Scott Arnold. She genuinely hoped she ran into him again some time in the near future.

Chapter 13

Diagnosis

Wally sat in a Queen Anne chair with oriental carpeting under his feet, facing a large mahogany desk. He was in Dr. Jackson Lipton's office. Any other patient would have been stuck waiting in an exam room, but as a professional courtesy, Dr. Lipton allowed Wally to wait in his office.

Wally allowed his eyes to survey the room, killing time as he waited for his friend Jack to join him with the results of his tests. A fully loaded bookcase hugged the wall on one side of the room. Jack's degrees and medical certificates hung in matching matted frames beside the bookcase. Directly in front of Wally, behind Jack's desk and leather chair, was an impressive and towering mahogany hutch. Jack had a very nice office. It screamed "success" for his doctor friend, and Wally was happy for him.

As Wally heard the doorknob jingle, he turned and watched as his friend opened the door and came into the room. The white-haired man was dressed in suit and tie, and he carried Wally's chart in his hands. "So what did you find, Jack? Am I going to live?" Wally asked with a nervous chuckle.

Dr. Lipton walked behind his desk and had a seat. Opening Wally's file across his desk, he looked from the report to Wally's eyes. With a slight slant to his lips, he said, "Wally, the good news is we did not find any brain tumors."

"Well, that's good to hear," Wally agreed, nodding. "So what exactly did you find, Jack?" he asked, maintaining intense eye contact, clenching and unclenching a fist.

"Well...the problem is...we didn't really find anything conclusive one way or the other," the doctor explained. He shuffled the papers in the folder, as if some answer would suddenly jump out at him.

"Okay..." Wally replied, a frown on his face. "So where do we go from here?"

Dr. Lipton scratched the back of his head, rendered a little cough, and said, "I think it might be a good idea for you to seek a second opinion, Wally..."

"Another neurologist?" Wally asked, his face scrunched in disagreement. "What are they going to find that you couldn't?"

"I...I, um...what I'm actually suggesting, Wally, is that you should seek counsel from a fellow colleague in your field," he clarified, squirming in his chair and glancing up and down.

"A psychiatrist?!" Wally probed, his eyes widening in surprise. "What...do you think I'm nuts, Jack? I'm not just imagining having severe headaches and memory lapses."

"No, I know you aren't, Wally," Dr. Lipton confirmed, slapping the arms of his chair with nervous energy. "I believe your pain and memory lapses are very real. The problem...as you know as a fellow physician...is that symptoms can indicate a variety of problems. Severe headaches and *extended* memory lapses could well be a sign of...of...well...D.I.D. for one thing," he pointed out, staring at his desk and scratching the top of his head. Jack did not like relaying this particular diagnosis, and he hoped he was wrong.

"D...I...D?!" Wally repeated, rocking forward in his chair. Staring into space and biting on his thumbnail, he questioned, "You seriously think I'm suffering from Dissociative Identity Disorder, Jack?"

"I don't know, Wally. That's just the point," Dr. Lipton replied with sympathetic eyes, tapping his index finger on his lips. "I'm only suggesting a second opinion from a psychiatrist. They can rule this other disorder out. I can't. In the meantime, I'm going to give you a prescription for some migraine medication. If taking the medication abates the problem with memory lapses, then you can pretty much figure migraines are your problem. If it doesn't…"

"Then I'm screwed!" Wally whined, filling in the blanks. He folded his arms across his stomach and bent his head as if he were going to be ill. He added in a mumble, "A psychiatrist can't be suffering from D.I.D. and seeing patients."

"Wally, we don't know that this is the case. I'm simply suggesting you see another doctor; that's all," he tried to reassure him.

Straightening back up in his seat, a pair of glistening furious eyes suddenly met Dr. Lipton's. The doctor was shocked to see how Wally's eyes had gone in a flash from panicked to angry.

"A psychiatrist seeing a psychiatrist…that would be rich!" Wally hissed, grinding his teeth.

Dr. Lipton averted his eyes from his friend's glare. He opened a drawer and pulled forth a prescription pad. Laying it on his desk on top of Wally's file, he reached to extract a pen from a tall, wooden pencil holder sitting on his desk. He quickly scribbled something on the pad and tore off the top sheet.

"Here's a prescription for some pretty potent migraine medication, Wally. Hopefully, this will solve the problem," Jack said, holding out the slip of paper toward his friend and colleague.

Dr. Lipton was surprised when Wally reached and snatched the piece of paper from his hand. Jack watched as Wally leapt to his feet. "I knew this would be a *huge* waste of time," he growled under his breath, turning and stomping toward the door.

"It was good seeing you again, Wally. Let's be optimistic and hope the medicine works," Dr. Lipton called after him with an encouraging half-smile.

"Stuff it, doc! I'll be just fine!" Wally snarled, reaching to grab the knob and jerking the door open.

Ignoring the stunned expression on Dr. Lipton's face, Wally rushed into the hallway, slamming the door behind him. Spying a red EXIT sign, he quickly hurried in that direction. A nurse jumped out of Wally's way as he raced forward with recklessness.

Wally decided with conviction, *I'll see a psychiatrist when hell freezes over!* He shoved open the door leading into the hallway. *I'm not going to let some nutcase neurologist mess up my life. I'm not going to let* anyone *do that. I'll be just fine. I didn't need to come here anyway*, he concluded.

He punched the down elevator button, but when the elevator did not immediately appear, Wally rushed off toward the door leading to the stairs. He wanted to get out of this building as quickly as possible.

Out of here and on with my life, he decided, taking the stairs two at a time. He was in control again now, and he would call the shots for his life. He had to take care of himself. If he did not, no one else would. He had learned this fact long ago. Wally continued to round the stairwell, eager to get to the door leading outside and to his freedom.

Chapter 14

Dinner

When Scott walked into the lobby of the Hendersonville Police Department, Sherri almost did not recognize him. Doing a double take, and walking toward him with a pleased smile, she said, "Well now...you certainly clean up well, Mr. Arnold. I appreciate you makin' good on your offer to buy me dinner some evenin', but you certainly don't have to take me anyplace fancy..."

"Not that I would mind taking you out for a fancy dinner, Sherri...," he said, returning her smile as he gave her a quick, approving perusal. As usual, Sherri was immaculate: makeup flawless, hair perfect, clothes unruffled. "But I'm actually dressed up for another reason," Scott informed her.

"And what might that be?" Sherri asked, averting her eyes. She was trying not to stare. Scott had never been a hard man to look at, but clean-shaven and in suit and tie, he was downright handsome. And she also could not help but notice that he smelled scrumptious. "Just what have you been up to, Scott?" she asked, looking him in the eye again.

"No good, I'm afraid," he admitted with sparking, mischievous eyes. Sinking his hands into his pant's pockets and rocking back on his heel, he began to whistle a little tune.

"'Fess up!" Sherri demanded with a chuckle, softly backhanding him in the stomach.

Scott stopped whistling and stood flat-footed again. Looking around at others walking about the lobby, he bent to whisper in Sherri's ear. "Why don't we talk about it in the van?" Then drawing away, he asked aloud, "Mind if I drive?"

"You were dyin' to drive my car the other day when I took you to the Nashvill' PD. So I guess I'll let you drive us around this time. At least it's stopped rainin'. I hate it when it rains for days on end like it has been," she said, looking out the glass front doors at the foggy, overcast evening. It was barely five o'clock, but the gloom made it dark.

"Well, I can't control the weather, but I can offer you a nice dinner. So shall we go?" Scott asked.

"I'll be right beside you," Sherri said, eager to be on the way.

Scott turned on his heel and Sherri, true to her word, fell into pace beside him.

"You outta here, Sherri?" a grey-haired, pot-bellied, uniformed policeman asked, as he stood in the open door, having just come into the building. He held open the door for Scott and Sherri.

As they passed him, Sherri replied, "Yeah, Dave. You take care. Have a good night. I'll see y'all tomorrow."

"See y'all," he said, releasing the door and continuing on into the lobby.

As Scott and Sherri walked across the parking lot to Scott's van, her low-heeled pumps clip-clopped on the asphalt. They both were careful to avoid puddles standing in the parking lot. As they approached the vehicle, Scott was tempted to walk Sherri to the passenger side and open her door for her. But he was not sure how she would take such action.

Sherri had a fierce independent streak, and Scott did not want to appear to be stepping on her toes. Plus, he did not want their dinner together to come across as a date. They were just two business colleagues sharing a harmless dinner.

"Um…the doors are unlocked," he told her as he headed to the driver's side.

Sherri nodded and walked toward the passenger door.

When they were both inside and had shut their doors, Scott turned the key in the ignition. An Eagles song blared through the speakers and drowned out the beeping of the seatbelt alert. "Sorry. I was jamming," Scott apologized, reaching to turn down the volume. Starting his van, the engine of the old Ford Econoline E-150 roared.

"I jam too when I'm alone in the car," Sherri admitted, snapping her seatbelt into place. "Although I'm more prone to be listenin' to Kenny Chesney."

"Yeah…Nashville area…country music…that sounds about right," Scott commented with a snicker, flashing a smile, and snapping his own seatbelt into place. "I have a CD in. I can switch to radio and find a country station if you like," he offered.

"No. That's alright. The Eagles are fine. You know… they started out doin' country," she pointed out with a knowing grin.

"Yeah…that they did," he agreed.

He turned on his headlights and backed out of the parking space then. As he pulled out of the parking lot, Sherri said, "Okay…enough with the stallin'…we're in the van now and we're on our way to dinner…so spill! What were you up to today in Nashvill'?"

"How'd you know I was in Nashville," he asked, glancing at her with a hint of surprise.

"I didn't know for sure until now, but I had a pretty good idea. You were nosin' around in the Robert Oaks case, weren't ya'?" she questioned.

Is she mad at me? Scott wondered. Sherri's eyes were hard to read. "Yes, I was," he confessed, gripping the steering wheel with both hands and looking out the windshield. "Is that a problem?" he asked, giving her a fleeting look.

"Not with me, it isn't," she replied, briefly meeting his eyes. "But you know it is with Lt. Gregory. Can you share with me exactly what you were up to?"

"Just gathering some names," Scott answered, focusing on the road again.

"The security guards' names," Sherri filled in the blanks, a trace of disapproval in her voice. "Scott, Geoffrey doesn't play around. You need to let the MNPD Homicide Squad do their job...."

"Now why wouldn't I let them do their job?" Scott interjected. Stopping at a red light, he gave Sherri his full attention. "I'm a private citizen. Last I heard, a private citizen has a right to talk to anyone he wants...."

"Unless it interferes in a homicide investigation," Sherri argued, her brown eyes darkening even more.

"I don't intend to *interfere* with the case, Sherri. But I do intend to gather some facts on my own. Hopefully, I can lend some support in solving this case. If Lt. Gregory doesn't want my information, maybe I'll pass it on to you, and you can share it with him."

"Thanks for puttin' me in the middle, Scott," Sherri snapped, looking out the front glass.

"I haven't put you in the middle of anything...yet," Scott pointed out. The traffic light changed to green, so he stepped down on the gas, revving the engine, and looked out at the highway ahead. "Look...if you don't want to be involved in this...that's fine. We should probably change the subject."

"Nice try, Yankee," Sherri said, studying his profile. His jaw was rigid. *He's aggravated with me*, she gathered. "Leavin' me out of the equation isn't goin' to stop you from snoopin' around. And if you do find anything...and as persistent as you are, you probably will...then it only makes sense for me to be in the loop. I can find a way to share the information with Geoffrey...as you've already assumed. Unlike you...Geoffrey likes me."

"For obvious reasons," Scott stated, looking her over with appreciative eyes.

"Thanks for the compliment," she said, her wide ruby lips widening in amusement.

Embarrassed, Scott quickly moved his eyes back to the street. He had allowed his eyes to linger a little too long. "Um... anyway...enough with the shop talk. What do you like to eat? You know the restaurants in this area. Or if you like, we can hop on the expressway and go into Nashville. The choice is yours. But you need to decide and give me directions, because the expressway is not that far away," he rambled, pointing with his hand at the road ahead.

Sherri stared at Scott's profile again with a grin. *He's nervous*, she noted, watching a nerve twitch in the side of his face. She was secretly glad the attraction between them was mutual. "Well...I know from watchin' you...um...inhale your breakfast the other mornin'...that you like greasy home cookin'..."

"It doesn't matter what I like. I can eat just about anything. Tonight is your night," Scott said, allowing himself another glance. "This is a 'thank you' dinner for sharing information with me on the Nashville homicide. Just tell me where to head."

"*Oh*...I could tell you where to go alright," she teased with a snicker.

"Hee...hee...hee," he mocked, rolling his eyes and shaking his head.

"Okay, okay...take a left at the next light," she began to direct.

Scott changed lanes and headed toward the intersection ahead. He was anxious to get to whatever restaurant Sherri chose for them. His stomach was grumbling, and he was looking forward to sharing a leisurely dinner with the charming lady beside him.

* * * *

When Scott pulled into the small, crowded parking lot of the restaurant, he laughed. A cracker-box, tan building, with a corral neon sign reading Edith's Diner across the top, stood in front of him. He pulled into a parking space and put the van in park.

"You're kidding, right? *This* is where you want to eat?" Scott asked, pointing to the building and grinning at Sherri. "You know...I do make money as a PI, Sherri. I could take you someplace nicer..."

"Hey...looks ain't everything. The food happens to be great! You'll see," Sherri swore, pulling the handle on her door and opening it. "Let's go. I'm starvin'!"

She hopped out of the van and shut the door. Scott opened his door and joined her in the parking lot, slamming his door as well. As they strolled toward the front door of the restaurant, the alluring smells caused Scott's mouth to water.

As Sherri entered the restaurant, she waved to a heavyset woman with grayish black hair pulled in a bun. This woman stood behind the counter at a cash register, making change for a man who was paying his bill. When she finished with the man, she called out, "Hey, Sherri," and smiled and waved.

"Hey, Edith," Sherry replied, before leading Scott by two tables that were occupied. There were only eight tables in the restaurant. There was also a counter with six stools. All but one of these stools was occupied, most of them by men.

There was an open table by the window, but Sherri headed to a table in the back instead. Nearby, an antique Wurlitzer jukebox played an old Johnny Cash song, "Walk the Line".

A middle-aged blonde, with a low-cut blouse and a short, black apron around the waist of her formfitting jeans, approached their table. She whipped a wet rag across the lime green, vinyl tablecloth, wiping away remnants of the last customer's meal. "Hey, Sher," she addressed Sherri.

"Hello, Wanda," Sherri replied. "I brought an outsider with me this evenin'. This is Scott Arnold, from Louisvill', KY. He thinks because this place is small, the food won't be any good. I'm lookin' forward to you guys provin' him wrong. Think you can do that for me?"

"You know we can, Sher," the woman seemed to promise. "You're in for a real treat, northerner," the waitress teased, eyeballing Scott with a grin.

"Looking forward to it," Scott told her with a chuckle. He noted the waitress's cleavage, her haggard face, and her piled-high hair.

"Good," the waitress said, before rushing away to gather some glasses of water, napkins, and silverware for them.

Scott directed his gaze at Sherri. He gave a chortle and shook his head. "You know, paybacks are hell, lady. I'd watch my step if I were you," he playfully warned.

"I stand warned," she said with a snicker.

The waitress returned. She set a small glass of iced water, silverware wrapped in a paper napkin, and a menu in front of each of them. "What can I get you both to drink?" she asked, taking out an order pad and a pen from her apron.

"Coke, for me," Scott answered, giving her another glance.

"I'll have lemonade," Sherri answered, watching Wanda record their drink orders.

"Comin' right up," the waitress said and hurried away.

Sherri took a sip of water. Looking across the table at Scott, curiosity got the better of her and she said, "I just have to know. What exactly does you bein' so dressed up today have to do with you gatherin' names?"

Scott opened his menu and studied it for a second before he replied with a snicker, "About the same thing you being a woman had to do with you getting information from Lieutenant Gregory the other day."

"So what did you do…smooze some girl to get the names?" Sherry inquired, tapping her fingers on her glass.

"That's about right," Scott admitted, glancing at his menu again.

The waitress returned and sat their drinks in front of them. "So have you decided what you'd like to order?" she asked, holding the order pad and pen in her hands again.

"What do you recommend?" Scott asked, looking to Sherri for guidance.

"Do you like country fried steak, green beans, and mashed 'taters?" Sherri asked.

"Yeah, I do," Scott answered.

"It figures," Sherri giggled. "Typical, good ole', home-cooked, country meal. Give us two of these dinners, Wanda," Sherri instructed.

The waitress jotted down the order. "Do you want white or dark gravy on your 'taters?" she directed her question at Scott. She seemed to know how Sherri wanted hers.

"Dark, please," he replied.

"Okay," she said, reaching to gather the menus. "I'll put in your order. It'll be out shortly," she told them, rushing away once more.

"Okay...now where were we?" Sherri asked, endeavoring to pick up on their conversation. "So you took advantage of some young girl and got her to give you the names of the security guards," she stated, taking a drink of her lemonade. It was perfect – not too tart and not too sweet.

"Hey, wait a sec!" Scott protested with a chuckle, holding up his hand, palm out. "I..." he began, pointing his index finger at himself, "...didn't take advantage of anyone. I merely asked a young lady for help. She could have said no, and that would have been the end of it."

He watched as a large man in coveralls wobbled over to the jukebox and dropped a quarter into the slot. A second later, "Crazy" by Patsy Cline began to play.

"Yeah, right! I could see this poor woman sayin' no to a handsome devil like you?" Sherri continued to banter with a knowing giggle.

"Hey…if her finding me cute added to her helpfulness, then how can I be faulted for that? Just like you can't be faulted that Lieutenant Gregory was wooed into submission by your pretty face," he pointed out with devilish eyes and a wide, wicked smile.

"Touché!" Sherri surrendered, drinking more of her lemonade. "So now that you have the names, where do you go from here?"

Scott reached in his pocket and pulled out the list. Unfolding the "While You Were Away" sheet, he gave the names greater notice. His eyes widened all at once, and then his brow furrowed.

"Scott…is everythin' okay?" Sherri asked. When he did not respond, she reached to touch his hand. He jumped at her touch. "What is it? Is Jeanette's name on the list?"

Looking up at her with a dazed expression on his face, he murmured, "N…no…but Deb…Debbie's is."

"*Debbie?*" she questioned, looking puzzled.

"Debbie Gray," Scott clarified, looking down at the sheet of paper again. He thought maybe his eyes had played tricks on him, but there it was again. Written in the receptionist's neat handwriting was the name *Debbie Gray*.

"*Eee*…that's an eerie coincidence," Sherri stated, squeezing Scott's hand.

"Coincidence?" Scott repeated in a questioning tone. "I don't think so," he surprised Sherri by stating. "Product of a sick mind, maybe. But definitely *not* a coincidence." There was fury in his voice and in his eyes. He pulled his hand away from Sherri's touch and balled it into a fist.

"You…you think that…that Jeanette is this Debbie Gray," Sherri put the pieces together, sitting back in her chair.

"You bet I do! It's Jeanette's final hurrah. Take on the identity of someone he murdered. What a plan!" Scott stated with assurance. He took a large swig of his soft drink to try and cool some of his growing outrage. "Realize something, Sherri…Jeanette handcuffed his first victim in Kentucky to a train track and watched her get mowed down. Then he cleverly made it look like the woman had committed suicide. He's devious and smart. But I've got him!"

"I really hope you're right, Scott," Sherri said, sympathetically studying his eyes.

"Well...there's one sure way to find out. I need to track down this...this Debbie... um...Debbie Gray."

Before he could continue – or make a dash for it like he felt like doing – the waitress appeared with their dinners. She sat a large, oval plate, overrun with food from corner to corner, in front of each of them. In the center of the table, she placed some extra napkins and a basket of freshly baked, crusty biscuits. Lastly, she laid the check facedown on the corner of the table. "Do ya' need anythin' else?" she asked.

It was Sherri that replied, "No...we're fine." Scott was still too preoccupied. He did not even seem interested in his food.

"Okay. I'll check back," Wanda told her and headed off.

"Scott," Sherri called. When he looked up at her, she continued, "I know you are rarin' to go chasin' after this...this Debbie character. I'm sure you are concoctin' how you can go about trackin' down her whereabouts..."

"You got that right," he agreed. His eyes were so serious they were black as coal. He still had not touched his food.

"But, can we at least enjoy a relaxin' dinner first? Who knows...I might be able to make a call and save you some time. You know MNPD has the addresses of the security guards," she reminded him.

"And you think Lt. Gregory is going to share that information with you?" Scott asked, his voice and his eyes relaying skepticism.

"As you pointed out...I have my ways of gettin' information out of people too," she confirmed, pinching a piece off of the top of a warm biscuit. "But first...I'm hungry. Can we eat?"

Scott had been famished before he extracted the piece of paper from his pocket and saw Debbie's name on the list. Now, his appetite had waned. However, as he looked across the table at Sherri, and saw her pick another piece off a biscuit and place it in her mouth, he realized he was being unsociable and unfair. This dinner was supposed to be a 'thank you' for all her help, and now, she was even offering to try and provide him further assistance. He needed to put his quest to find Jeanette on hold for another half an hour or so and enjoy sharing dinner with the lady across from him.

"I'm sorry," Scott apologized. "You're right. I brought you here to have a relaxing dinner, and that is exactly what we are going to do," he told both himself and Sherri.

"Good!" Sherri chirped. "Now dig in. I'm eager to see what you think of the food."

Scott unwrapped his silverware from his napkin. He placed his napkin in his lap and stuck his fork into a steak smothered in white gravy. He carved off a piece of the meat with his knife. Sticking it in his mouth, he savored the taste for a second, "Oh-um...it's good," he told Sherri with a pleased grin, letting the beef melt in his mouth before he began chewing.

"I'm glad you like it," Sherri said, returning his smile.

She also unwrapped her utensils and dug into her own food, happy to have abated Scott's ire and unrest for a few moments. She looked forward to a peaceful dinner now. She also looked forward to getting Scott the information he needed to track down Debbie Gray. He did not know it yet, but she intended to follow up on this lead with him. She would be there to support him with legal backup if he was right, or with emotional comfort if he was wrong.

Chapter 15

Wiles

They had just finished eating. Wanda came and removed their dirty dishes and silverware. She returned a few moments later to refill their drinks one last time and to offer them dessert. When they both declined her dessert offer, she said, "You guys have a great evenin'!" Then on a personal note, she added, "Sher, I'm sure we'll be seein' ya' again soon."

"No doubt," she confirmed with a snicker. "You take care, Wanda."

Wanda nodded and scurried away, moving on to wait on other tables and solicit other tips.

Sherri extracted her purse from the floor, reached inside and pulled out her cell phone. "Let's see what information I can get for you," she said to Scott.

"Sherri, you don't have to do that," Scott cautioned her.

He did not want to see her get into any kind of trouble. He remembered all too well all of the hoops one had to jump through because of being part of a police squad. And he knew he could track down Debbie Gray's address on his own. It might take him a bit longer, but he could gather the details by himself if need be.

"I want to do this for you, Scott," Sherri assured him, punching numbers into the phone. "Just sit back and relax and watch how I use my charm to get information. As you pointed out, you're not the only one that can play these games," she said with a knowing smile, placing the phone up to her ear.

A few seconds later, Scott listened to her request, "Sergeant Nelson Riley, please."

Who? Scott wondered with a wrinkled brow.

"N*e*lson," he listened to Sherry coo. "How are you this evenin'? This is Sergeant Sherri Ball, from Hendersonvill'."

"Hi, Sherri," Nelson replied. "What can I do for you this evening?"

"Well...I have a question for you...and I'm hopin' you can help me out," she relayed.

"Ask away, and I'll see what I can do," Nelson offered.

"Okay," she agreed. "Here's the deal. You guys are workin' the Robert Oaks homicide, and we are workin' the Jack Jordan slayin' in Hendersonvill'. The two crimes seem to have a common link..."

"Yeah...so?" he stated, a hint of impatience in his voice. "Was there a question in there somewhere?"

"Comin' right up. I know you are a busy man...what with bein' at the Central Patrol Precinct right in front of the Gaylord and all...," Sherri stated with a friendly chuckle. Glancing at Scott with a smile, she continued, "Here's my dilemma...it's come to light that one of the security guards you guys questioned, a...Debbie Gray, might have known our vic'. So obviously, we need to follow up on this lead. I could go over to the Gaylord and get this woman's address. But I thought...heck...why bother with that? You guys are bound to have that information at your fingertips. I know how thorough you guys are. I just need to get an address for this Debbie Gray. That's all. You can help me out with that, can't you, Nelson? Save me a trip to the Gaylord?"

"I could give you the address...yeah..."

"Oh...that would be grand! I really would appreciate that, Nelson. You are such a great guy! It's always a pleasure workin' with you guys!" Sherri went overboard with mushiness.

Scott grinned and rolled his eyes.

"Whoa...slow down one cotton-pickin' minute," Nelson said, sounding irritated. "I *could* give you the address, Sherri... but I'm wonderin'...if this security guard has a tie to your vic' and had access to our vic', then shouldn't MNPD be the one showin' up at her house askin' questions?

"You might be on to somethin' there, Nelson," Sherri agreed, quickly adding, "But...I'm not sure how credible my lead is. That's why I want to ask Debbie Gray some questions. If my lead pans out, then I...of course...would pass along whatever information I gather to you guys. I'd just be doin' the legwork; that's all. Hendersonvill' always takes a backseat to MNPD in investigations. We're just the little guy on the block. We bow to your expertise. But as I said, I know you guys are extremely busy, and I don't want you wastin' your time questionin' this woman and have our lead not pan out. I also don't want you to have mud on your face, runnin' with a lead that isn't credible."

"Well..." he said, heaving a sigh. "If you're not even sure your lead is credible, then I guess it does make sense to let you do some legwork first. Hang on a sec. I'll get you that address."

"Thank you so much, Nelson! You're a peach!" she gushed again. She pulled the phone away from her ear, put her hand over the mouthpiece and shared a laugh with Scott, telling him, "I'll have that address for you in just a sec." Then Sherri placed the phone back up to her ear and waited patiently.

A moment later, Nelson said, "Sherri."

"Yeah," she replied.

"The address you're lookin' for is...get this...5555 Cherokee Road. Right in Hendersonville. Your neck of the woods."

"Practically at my backdoor," Sherri told him. "Thanks again, Nelson. I owe you big!"

"Just be sure and call me back and let me know what you find out," he instructed.

"Will do!" she promised. "You have a great night!"

"You too," he said.

Sherri pushed the *End* button on her phone then, disconnecting the call. "Yeah!" she exclaiming, shaking her fists in victory in front of her. Tossing her phone back into her purse, Sherri said to Scott, "Are you ready for this?"

"You know I am," he replied, sitting on the edge of his seat, rubbing his hands together. "What's her address?"

"Debbie Gray lives right here in Hendersonville," she shared. "5555 Cherokee Road. That's right off the Johnny Cash Pkwy."

"I'll be camped out at her doorstep," Scott announced. He pulled forth his wallet, pulled out three one-dollar bills and tossed them – folded – on the table. Then he scooped up the check, and leaped to his feet. "Are you ready to go?"

"Yeah," Sherri answered, pushing her chair back and also standing. "You aren't goin' over there now, are you?" she asked with concern.

"I plan on driving by there this evening…yeah," Scott admitted. "I need to scope out the area. Find a place to park my van and do some surveillance. I need to catch Jeanette…or Debbie as he's known now…as he leaves his house. I'll bet ten-to-one that there is a three-year-old girl living in that house too. You better be ready to make a call to Nelson and the MNPD for real, because they will soon have a serial murderer to bring in," Scott said with confidence.

"Well…if you are plannin' on drivin' by there now, I can show you the way," Sherri offered, struggling to keep up with him as he dashed for the cash register.

"You don't have to do that, Sherri. You've involved yourself enough just by getting the address for me. I really appreciate that. Seems I owe you another dinner. Next time, I'll pick the place…someplace a little more upscale…not that the food wasn't absolutely delicious," he assured her with a confirming grin.

"Glad to hear ya' enjoyed the food," the woman behind the counter said, giving him a smile. She was missing one of her front bottom teeth. The woman took the check and a twenty-dollar bill from Scott's outstretched hand. "Good to see ya', Sherri. Nice to see you out on a date too. 'Bout time," the old woman added with a twinkle in her eye and a conspiring snicker.

"*Oh...*" Sherri giggled, her face coloring a little as Scott looked from Edith to her. "This...it wasn't a date," she clarified.

"Why the heck not?" Edith demanded to know. "He's darn good-lookin'!" she pointed out, as if Sherri had not noticed. She handed Scott his change – one dollar bill and some change.

Scott's turn to be embarrassed, he chuckled and said, "Thanks," referring to both the change and her compliment.

"Bye, Edith," Sherri said, turning to rush for the door.

"Bye, Sherri. See ya' soon. You kids enjoy the rest of your evenin'," she said and giggled again.

"Sorry 'bout that," Sherri apologized when she and Scott were out in the parking lot.

"About what?" he questioned. "I have no problem with people thinking I might be out on a date with you," he surprised both Sherri and himself by saying. He had not meant to say these words, but Scott knew they were true.

"*O...*kay," Sherri replied with a nervous giggle and picked up her pace toward the van. She really did not know how to respond to Scott's last comment. *Regardless of his last comment, we are* not *on a* date, she reminded herself. *I'm just helping him bring a killer to justice.*

Sherri went around to the passenger side of the van, opened the door, climbed in, and shut the door behind her. Scott joined her inside, shutting his own door. "Did I make you uncomfortable with my comment about dating you?" Scott asked.

"A little," Sherri admitted, looking down into her lap. "As you may have gathered from Edith's comment, I haven't dated much since my divorce. I was married almost eight years...straight out of high school, and even though he cheated on me…numerous times…I still feel married after bein' divorced for more than a year. How crazy is that?" Sherri asked, glancing at Scott.

"No crazier than being in love with a ghost," Scott admitted, looking away from Sherri and clutching the steering wheel. "I haven't been out on a date since Debbie died…over a year and a half ago," he confessed, directing his gaze toward her again.

"I'm sorry," Sherri said. "It's obvious you loved her a great deal. She was a very lucky lady."

"I always thought it was the other way around," Scott said, looking away again. "Anyway…maybe it's time we both got back out there again. Maybe it wouldn't be such a bad idea if we went on a date or two," he proposed, meeting her eyes again.

"I…I don't know," Sherri replied, looking down into her lap again. "I have my daughter to think of…"

"Hey…I'm not proposing marriage here," Scott said with a chuckle. "Although it's admirable that you put your daughter first. The more I get to know you, the more I like about you, Sherri," Scott indicated again.

Sherri met his eyes. She suddenly was filled with the most insane temptation to scoot across the seat, put her arms around his neck, and kiss him. "Uh…Scott," she murmured, lowering her eyes. "We…uh…we…aren't we goin' to go by that address?"

"In other words…change the subject, right?" he said with a knowing laugh. "I get it." He placed the key in the ignition and started the van. The engine roared, the seatbelt alert beeped, and the song "Peaceful Easy Feeling" played from the CD. "Let's head out. We'll keep it strictly business tonight. Alright, Sergeant Ball?"

"I think that's best. At least for now," she answered, breathing a sigh of relief, as she snapped her seatbelt into place. *The seatbelt will protect me in more ways than one tonight – It'll keep me on this side of the car*, she mused.

Scott secured his own seatbelt, turned on the headlights, and shifted into drive, pulling the van out of the parking space. Heading toward the street, he inquired, "So which way do I turn when I leave the parking lot."

"Right," she answered, pointing.

Scott pulled the van out onto the highway, heading right as Sherri had directed him, eager to get to the address of Debbie Gray – the beginning to a long awaited end for him.

Chapter 16

The Plan

Scott followed Sherri's directions and drove past the house at 5555 Cherokee Road. It was a medium-sized, brick ranch.

"Scott, you just passed the house," Sherri pointed out, turning her head as she watched the house disappear behind her.

"Yeah, I know," he told her.

He drove up the street a few more houses. Then he turned into a driveway, put the van in reverse, and backed out onto the street once more. He put the van in drive and headed in the direction of Debbie's house once more.

"I'm going to drive back by it…slower this time. Keep your eagles eyes peeled. Look for lights that are on in the house, a car in the driveway, and kid's toys," he instructed, glancing over at her.

"Okay," she agreed. She turned her head and looked out the side window.

As Scott drove past the house again, Sherri carefully surveyed the residence and its surroundings. She shared her observations with Scott. "There isn't a car in the driveway, but it could likely be in the garage. There's a small Big Wheel with pink handles by the side porch…I'd guess this is a little girl's. And there's a light on in the house…in the back…middle of the house."

"And I bet the room with the light on is the kitchen," Scott theorized. "It's a little past six o'clock," he added, pointing to the white digital **6:07** on the face of the radio. He had switched from CD to radio when he and Sherri had left the restaurant, allowing her to enjoy some country music for the drive to Debbie Gray's house. "Perfect time for Debbie and her daughter to be sharing a little dinner," Scott pointed out.

"The little girl you mentioned is this monster's daughter?" Sherri asked, her eyes widening with surprise. When Scott had revealed that Jeanette had a little girl with him, Sherri had assumed that this man had kidnapped a child.

"By adoption…yes. That is…after he killed both the girl's parents," he explained, squeezing the steering wheel.

"Egad, Scott!" Sherri exclaimed, shaking her head. "I really do hope that this Debbie Gray is your Jeanette. She definitely needs to be taken off the street…and taken off the street ASAP."

"That's what I've been telling you," Scott reminded her, giving her a knowing glance. He stopped the van at the stop sign at the end of the street, shifting it into park, and he turned to face Sherri.

"So what are you goin' to do now?" she asked, studying his eyes for clues.

"I'm going to take you back to the police station to your car," he announced, toying with the keychain dangling from the ignition – a University of Louisville cardinal.

"What? Why?" Sherri questioned. Her straight lips and creased forehead relayed her displeasure and confusion. "Aren't you goin' to check things out back there?" she asked, pointing back toward the house.

"What am I supposed to do? Pull in her driveway, walk up to her front door, ring the doorbell, and ask her if she remembers me?" His voice was loaded with sarcasm as he asked these questions, and his eyes were intense.

"So what's your plan then?" Sherri asked, staring him down. "Don't tell me you don't have one swirlin' around in that head of yours," she said, tapping her temple. "I've got your number now, Scott…what with how you snuck around and got the names of the security guards today. Why don't you let me help? I've been involved thus far. And if you can ID this Debbie as Jeanette, then I have the authority to get an arrest warrant. You're goin' to need my help anyway," she pointed out with a calculating smirk.

"Yeah, at some point, I'll need your help," Scott conceded, releasing the keychain and picking at the cloth seat beside him with nervous energy. "But right now, there is not a lot you can do. I need to set up surveillance close to the house and watch for her to come out. I can take photos…hopefully of both her and the girl, and then I can study them to see if I can ID her."

"But, Scott…you said yourself…since our shoe mould showed our perp weighs 175 or 180 pounds…that Jeanette has more than likely put on twenty-five pounds. Who knows how else she has altered her appearance. She may be very hard to ID from a photo," Sherri argued.

"This could be true," Scott had to agree, rubbing his smooth chin and pursing his lips. He was giving her argument due consideration.

"I know you don't want to waste time. Your perp has never seen me before. I could easily approach her."

"Yeah, and do what?" Scott asked, his face scrunching up. "You can't question him, Sherri. If Jeanette gets wind that the cops are sniffing around, he will run again. I have no doubt of that. And if he could steal Debbie's identity, then he could easily change identities again. This explains why Jeanette's trail went so cold," Scott concluded.

In his side mirror, he spied a car coming up behind the van. Scott turned on his flashers, rolled down his window, and motioned with his arm for the car to go around. "We better be going," he told Sherri. "If a bunch of people in this neighborhood spy my van sitting around, then when I come back to set up surveillance, they might call the cops on me…"

"I could see them doin' this anyway," Sherri argued. "After all…you have out of state plates. If this was a work van parked along the street, it would have Tennessee plates."

"Your arguments are sound. Maybe I'll go rent a van and set up shop," Scott spoke his thoughts aloud. His eyes darted to and fro as he began to plan.

"Or..." Sherri said, touching his hand to make sure she had Scott's full attention. When he looked her in the eye, she continued, "We could put our heads together and think of some way for me to approach this woman. LMPD has Jeanette's DNA, correct?"

"Ye...ah," Scott slowly confirmed, his eyes turning questioning again.

"If I can get a DNA sample from this Debbie Gray, then we can see if the two match. If they don't, then obviously she isn't the same person. But if they do..."

"Then you'll be getting that arrest warrant," Scott finished her sentence with an admiring smile. "So how do we do this?" he asked, sounding enthusiastic about her help for the first time.

"I don't know yet, but I'm sure between the two of us we can come up with a plan. Why don't you take me back to the police department, and then you can follow me to my house. We'll continue this discussion there," she suggested.

"You...you want me to come to your house?" Scott asked with noted surprise. "What about your daughter?"

"She's with her dad. I won't have her till tomorrow night. So we would have the place all to ourselves. I can't think of a better place to plan strategy; can you?" she asked, staring into his eyes with conviction.

"Works for me," Scott agreed, turning off his flashers, starting the van, and shifting it into drive.

Scott surveyed the cross-street facing them in both directions. Seeing no cars approaching, he moved his foot from the brake to the gas. He stepped down on the pedal, causing the engine to zoom, and sent the van on its way to the police station.

Chapter 17

Morning

The delightful aroma of bacon met Scott's nose. He opened his eyes and surveyed dim, unfamiliar surroundings: a brass vanity with a tiffany lamp, a chest-of-drawers, a bookcase filled with books and collectibles, and a sheered window revealing the darkness outside. Slowly, he became conscious of where he resided. He was in the spare bedroom at Sherri's house. She had invited him to spend the night after their planning session the evening before.

Scott pitched off a flowery-patterned down comforter and sat up in bed. Sliding his legs over the side, he stretched and yawned, forcing his mind to fully awaken. He was not sure exactly what time it was. There was a clock on the wall, but it was not lighted, so he could not see where the hands pointed.

Scott guessed it was early morning, since he had told Sherri the night before that he wanted to get an early start. That was one of the reasons she had invited him to stay. She thought it foolish for him to have to pay for a hotel room, and driving back to Louisville would have been even sillier.

Scott finally conceded to her hospitality, and now, as the smell of bacon had him salivating, he was glad he had. He stood and guided his bare feet across the cool, creaking hardwood floor to a closed door. Turning the knob, he pulled the door open and made his way into the sparsely lit hall. The plush carpet in the hallway hugged and warmed his feet as he padded to the bathroom.

Scott switched on the light in the bathroom and blinked as his eyes adjusted to its brightness. As he stepped inside, the beige tile floor chilled his feet. Scott shut the door and stepped over to the toilet. Raising the lid, he emptied his bladder. Flushing the toilet, he started away. Then it struck him once more, *You're not at home. You're at Sherri's house.* He spun and lowered the toilet seat.

Walking to the sink, he turned on the water and let it run a few moments, waiting for it to warm. Washing his hands, he cupped some of the water in his palms, lowered his head, and ran it over his face. Looking at himself in the mirror, he also ran his wet fingers through his hair, taming his bed head a bit.

A toothbrush and some toothpaste still laid by the side of the sink from the night before. The toothbrush was one Sherri had given him to use. He picked up the tube of toothpaste and unscrewed the top, laying it on the vanity. Then he picked up the toothbrush in his other hand and squeezed some of the toothpaste onto the bristles. He proceeded to brush away his morning breath.

Sliding his feet sideways, Scott reached for a metal hanger on the closet door, where his clothes hung. His belt buckle jangled as he raised his suit jacket and dress shirt up and slid his dress pants from the bottom.

Scott had slept in white boxer briefs and a T-shirt. Sliding his dress pants over his boxers, he tucked in the T-shirt and at last, turned to head out of the bathroom. He would get fully dressed after breakfast, but for now, his stomach was screaming for him to join Sherri in the kitchen, and he felt he had made himself presentable.

As Scott opened the bathroom door, he came almost nose to nose with Sherri. "Mornin'," she said with a glorious smile, taking a sip from a Garfield coffee mug.

"Good morning," Scott replied. He noted that Sherri was dressed in a long, pink, terrycloth robe with matching fuzzy slippers; her hair was ruffled, and she did not have on any makeup. He still thought she looked adorable.

"I heard you stirrin' around. I just came to tell you that breakfast is ready whenever you are," Sherri told him, stepping back, so Scott could vacate the bathroom.

"I've been ready for breakfast ever since the smell woke me up," Scott confessed, joining her in the hall. "I thought you didn't eat big breakfasts."

"Normally…I don't," she admitted, taking another drink from her cup. Scott could see steam rolling off the top, and the scent of the fresh brew pleased his nostrils. He could not wait to get his hands on a cup of Sherri's coffee either.

"So why today? Just because I'm here you didn't have to go to any extra trouble," Scott told her. They were meandering up the hallway toward the kitchen.

"Maybe I wanted to go to the extra trouble," Sherri said, demurely lowering her eyes. Then she revealed with a chuckle, "It's kind of nice to cook for someone again who doesn't still eat baby food with their meals."

"Hey…how do you know that I don't still enjoy a jar or two of baby food with my meals from time to time?" Scott teased with a snicker.

"Well…I have plenty of it in the cupboards if that's the case," Sherri shared, flashing him another smile.

They turned into the kitchen then. Scott's mouth began to water as he spied scrambled eggs and bacon in skillets on the stove. He walked over to the coffee maker across the room first. Pouring himself a cup of the great-smelling brew, he took a sip and smiled at Sherri.

"I don't see how you can drink it black like that. But I'm glad to see that you seem to be enjoyin' it," she said, noting his grin. "Help yourself to all the eggs and bacon you want too."

"Have you already eaten?" he asked.

"No…guests go first," she said.

"Well…where I come from…a lady goes first," he contradicted. "Please…fix yourself a plate, and then I'll follow."

"Goodness...look who's so chivalrous this mornin'," Sherri joked. But she grabbed a plate and stepped up to the food, filling her plate. She was in a good mood. She liked having Scott there. It felt right.

After Scott filled his plate as well, the two sat down at the kitchen table and had a quiet, relaxing breakfast together. They took turns sharing sections from a local newspaper, and they both eased into the morning.

When Scott had finished his breakfast and his second cup of coffee, he laid down the sports section and tapped on the back of the Features section that Sherri held in front of her face. When Sherri lowered the paper, Scott smiled at her and said, "Thanks."

"For what?" she asked. The paper crinkled and popped as she folded it and laid it on the table in front of her.

"For everything. For helping with the case. For letting me stay here last night. And for fixing me such a *delicious* breakfast! You're a great lady, Sherri," he praised, his grin widening.

"Now it's my turn to say thanks," she replied, laughing and lowering her eyes in embarrassment.

"I've enjoyed getting to know you, Sherri," Scott said, then added, "And...I look forward to getting to know you a *lot* better."

When Sherri's eyes met Scott's admiring stare, she had to look away. "*O*...kay," she replied, chuckling again. She pushed her chair back and stood. "It's about time we got our day under way, don't you think? You said you wanted to get an early start, and it's already almost six a.m.," she rambled, reaching to pick up Scott's plate along with her own. Sherri walked over to the sink, taking a second to rinse both plates. Then she left them stacked in the sink basin.

When she turned, she found herself face to face with Scott. "We do need to get our day under way," he confirmed. "But not until I do this," he said, cupping her face with his hands and bringing his lips to hers.

Sherri instantly responded. They stood kissing for several minutes, lost in the moment. When they finally parted, Sherri was dazed and Scott was aroused beyond reason. He grabbed hold of the ties to her robe and asked in a husky voice, "I'm wondering…do you have on anything under this robe?"

"Y…yeah…I have…I have on…" she stuttered. Then, clutching Scott's hands, she said in a panicked voice, "Scott, we need to slow things way down here."

Seeing the fear and pleading in her eyes, Scott released her robe and backed away a step. "Sorry," he said, exhaling loudly. "You're right," he begrudgingly agreed, raking a hand through his hair. "It was just…your kisses rattled me. You're some kisser, lady!" he exclaimed with a nevous laugh, his eyes still gleaming with desire.

"I think you are just deprived," Sherri downplayed with a chuckle, moving her shaky legs sideways, to put more distance between them. Her mind was screaming, "caution", but her body was shouting, "surrender". She wanted Scott, and she wanted him badly. "We…uh…we should get ready to leave," she suggested, pointing to the archway leading out of the kitchen and moving farther in that direction. "If…if you want to take a shower, there are clean towels in the bathroom closet," she told him.

"I definitely need to take a shower," Scott said. Then he added with dancing eyes, "A cold one."

"That sounds like a really good idea," Sherri agreed. "You head to the bathroom in the hallway. I'll head to the one in the bedroom. We'll meet back in the kitchen when we're both ready to go," Sherri instructed in a monologue, turning to head across the kitchen.

When she turned, in the hallway, she found Scott facing her and smiling in amusement. She walked away without another word. *He's cute. God, he's cute! But I've got to keep my head about me!* Sherri warned herself as she escaped down the hall to her bedroom. Once in her bedroom, she shut and locked the door – closing out Scott and any further temptation. The moment had passed.

Chapter 18

Sighting

As the skies brightened and darkness abated, Scott's van became more noticeable to the eye. It was parked beside a curb across the street from Debbie Gray's house. He had long ago climbed in the back of the vehicle and spied out a dark-tinted window through a slit in the curtains. He watched. He waited.

Finally, about seven-thirty, he saw Debbie's garage door rolling open. Then Scott sighted a heavyset, dark-haired woman walking out from the back of the house toward the garage. She had a small child by the hand – a little girl. *Bingo!* Scott thought with utmost exhilaration, expelling a gurgle of satisfied laughter.

Scrambling into the front of the van, Scott stabbed his key into the ignition. His keychain chimed as he rotated his wrist with a jerk. The engine started and a morning traffic report blared from the radio. He reached to turn the volume down, while still intently watching Debbie's driveway. Her car began to clear the garage and make its way up the driveway.

Scott stepped down ever so gently on the gas pedal. He did not want the engine to rev and draw attention to him. Scott slowly propelled the van back a few houses. He did not want to be in Debbie's way when she backed out. The last thing he needed was for her to accidentally back into his van.

As Scott dropped the van back into drive, he saw that Debbie had already cleared her driveway and was heading up the street toward the stop sign. He began to tail her. Scott's front windows were also tinted – as dark as the law would allow – so it was not easy for another driver to clearly make him out. But he still kept a careful distance behind Debbie's car. He was not about to take any chances.

Scott mulled over the radical difference in Jeanette's appearance. Regardless, he was still convinced that this *Debbie Gray* was indeed *Jeanette Peterson*. As he continued to follow her, he noted that his heart was racing and the palms of his hands were sweating. *So close!* His mind screamed.

Scott had to fight to keep from flying up beside Debbie's car and forcing her off the road. He wanted to confront her right here and now. *Cool it! You'll get her. Stick to the plan*, he told himself, dropping back in traffic, but keeping Debbie clearly in sight.

* * * *

About an hour later, Sherri's phone rang and she reached to pick it up. "S*ergeant B*all," she answered.

"Sergeant Ball," the dispatch officer's voice repeated. "There is a Scott Arnold here to see you."

"Oh…okay," she replied. "Tell him to come on up and I'll meet him in the hall," Sherri instructed.

"Will do," the officer responded.

Sherri hung up her phone and rolled back her chair. "I'll be back in a few, Newton," she said to her partner. "I need to meet with someone for a moment."

"Okay…whatever," Newton replied, barely giving her a glance.

Newton was a middle-aged man that wore checkered shirts and ties that were too short. He also had a bad comb over and dark, large-rimmed glasses. Currently, he was engrossed in working on his PC. Sherri listened to the *click…click…click* as Newton continued to tap his fingers in a smooth motion on his keyboard.

Sherri stood and headed for the door leading out of the area and into the hall. She was anxious to hear what Scott had to say. She was also looking forward to seeing him again, even though they had only been parted a few hours. *What's happening to me!* she wondered in panic, taking a deep breath to settle her jitters. Sherri stepped out into the hall and awaited Scott's welcome appearance.

A moment later, the elevator doors opened, and the sight of Scott's tall frame, shiny black hair, piercing dark eyes, and gleaming white teeth made Sherri's legs weak. In a way, she was glad her legs felt rubbery, because this strange sensation prevented her from dashing forward and engulfing Scott in her arms. She found herself unconsciously fingering her lips as mental images of their heated kisses from that morning replayed in her mind.

When Sherri realized what she was doing and that she was staring at Scott, she dropped her hand, joining it to her other at her waist, and averted her eyes. "Is there some reason for your visit…and…that smile?" she asked breathily, glancing at Scott again.

"You bet there is," he chirped. "Can we go to the conference room and talk?"

"Sure," Sherri agreed.

She turned and began making her way down the hall. Scott fell into pace beside her. "So…how has your day been so far?" he asked, sounding both interested and like he was making friendly conversation.

"It's been fine," Sherri answered, allowing her eyes to only make fleeting contact.

Her heart was hammering and she felt lightheaded. She forged onward toward the conference room. Sherri focused on the linoleum and the sound of their heels tip-tapping on the floor. She glanced at closed office doors as they passed. She noted the dim glow and the humming of the fluorescent lights leading the way along the passageway.

Arriving at last at the conference room, Sherri opened the door and flipped the wall switch to illuminate the room. She rushed over to the nearest chair. It scratched along the floor as she jerked it away from the table and took a quick seat in it. She quickly pushed it up to the table.

Scott pulled out the chair across from her and also had a seat. "Are you okay, Sherri?" he asked. He noted she looked pale, even though, unlike this morning, she now wore makeup.

"Yeah. I'm fine," she lied, looking down at the table. Making eye contact, with straight-lined lips, she asked, "What did you want to talk to me about?" She was getting right down to business. Sherri wanted no more personal talk between her and Scott. She needed to settle her nerves and get her head back together.

Scott could tell Sherri was bothered by something and he had a good idea what that *something* was. He wanted to talk about their earlier intimate encounter, but he sensed now was not the time or the place. Right now, their primary focus needed to be on catching Jeanette.

"I'm more convinced than ever that Debbie Gray is Jeanette Peterson," he revealed with a wide smile.

"What makes you think this?" Sherri questioned, fidgeting in her seat as she fought to ignore his handsome grin and the butterflies in her stomach.

"Debbie's heavier, and her hair is longer, straighter, and a different shade. But she's the same height as Jeanette, and she walked out of the house holding the hand of a little girl. A little girl about the same age Jeanette's little girl would be. Coincidence? I think not," Scott relayed, tapping his hands together.

"So what's your plan?" Sherri asked, linking her hands and leaning back in her chair.

"Debbie is at work right now. I followed her from her house, to a preschool, and then on to the Gaylord. Then I came here. We obviously need to get you in front of her," Scott pointed out, scratching the five o'clock shadow on his chin and scrunching up his face.

"So do you want me to go over to the Gaylord now? I'm sure I could ask a few questions and track her down," Sherri assured him.

She placed her hands on the arms of her chair as if she were about to push it back and stand up. Sherri was anxious to track this woman down as well. If she could get a DNA sample, they could confirm one way or another whether this woman was the dangerous killer, Jeanette Peterson, or not.

"I...I know we decided you should approach her at work. But I'm really starting to have second thoughts about this plan now," Scott shared, placing his elbow on the chair arm and leaning his head on his hand.

"Why? What's botherin' you about this plan now?" Sherri questioned, her eyes narrowing in bewilderment.

"I know it's a long shot, but what if someone from the MNPD happens to show up there at the same time? If they see you questioning Debbie, they might feel the need to do the same. I don't want to take the chance of cluing Debbie in – in any way – that the cops are on their trail. She'll be gone in a flash."

"Okay...so what's a better plan?" Sherri asked, releasing the arms of the chair, leaning forward and tapping on the table with her fingernails.

"I don't know," Scott admitted, exhaling in frustration. He noted Sherri looked impatient. He was glad to see that she wanted to catch this killer as greatly as he did.

"Look...Scott...we can tiptoe around this thing and try to look for a," she held up her fingers making quote signs. "'Safe plan'. Or, we can run with what we've already decided and possibly garner some evidence today to put this killer away. I for one don't want to drag our feet on this. I think we should go with our original plan. The sooner the better," she argued, folding her hands on the table in front of her, as if to say, 'I rest my case'.

Scott's face furrowed again as he gave serious consideration to Sherri's argument. He did not want to drag his feet on this case either. He wanted to jump in with both feet and run with their plan. They needed a DNA sample, and they needed it ASAP, and he trusted Sherri's judgment. Jeanette had gone free far too long.

"Okay," he finally concurred, straightening up in his chair and nodding his head. His lips curved upward in approval.

"Good," Sherri said, leaning back in her chair. "When do you want to go over there?"

"The way I see it...if we are going to do it...let's do it!" Scott answered. His chair screeched as he pushed it back and stood. "Ready to get this show on the road, lady? Can you leave right now?" he questioned, rubbing his hands together.

"Did you take any pictures of this woman, so I know what she looks like?" Sherri asked, pushing her own chair back and standing.

"Come on, Sherri," Scott said with a chuckle. "Who do you think you're dealing with here...an amateur? Taking photos of unsuspecting victims is what I do for a living now. I got some great shots of Ms. Debbie Gray, both at the preschool and in the parking garage," he shared with a proud grin.

"Good," Sherri replied. "Let's roll on this," she said.

Turning and opening the door to the conference room, she stepped into the hall. When Scott walked past her, she reached to turn off the lights in the room and shut the door. Then they both hurried up the hallway. They were on an vital mission...together.

Chapter 19

Face to Face

Sherri walked right past the police precinct in the front of the Gaylord Entertainment Center. She opened the next door down and strolled past a male security guard, who hardly gave her any notice. The security guard was preoccupied at his computer terminal.

Sherri glanced at pictures hanging on the wall behind him as she strolled past. The pictures were obviously of stars who had performed at the Gaylord. Sherri also took a brief glimpse down a hallway directly ahead of her. It was lit by bright, swirling, track lighting all along the ceiling, and pictures of Nashville's hockey team – The Predators – lined the walls.

As if Sherri belonged in this building, she headed directly to the elevators off to the left. Scott had told her which floor the Human Resources Department was on. Stepping on an elevator, she pushed the appropriate number and waited for the elevator doors to close and the elevator to rise.

When she arrived on her floor, she stepped off the elevator and into a quiet and carpeted hallway. On the door at the far end of the vacant hall was a brass plate that read 'Human Resources'. Sherri steered her legs in that direction.

Arriving at the end of the hall, Sherri opened the door in front of her. She spied an overweight blond-haired lady sitting at a desk behind a granite counter. Sherri guessed this woman was Adrianna, the lady Scott had gathered information from. She certainly fit his description. Sherri approached the counter.

"May I help you?" the woman asked, halting her typing and turning from her computer to give her full attention to her guest.

"I hope so," Sherri answered. Pulling forth a badge from the pocket of her slacks, she held it up where the receptionist could see it, revealing, "I'm detective Ball from the Hendersonville PD. I need to speak to one of your security guards."

"This is about the murder right outside this building, isn't it?" Adrianna questioned, pursing her lips.

"No," Sherri replied. "This is actually about a murder that occurred in Hendersonvill'. But we have reason to think it might tie in with your Nashvill' murder."

"Oh!" Adrianna responded, sounding surprised and unsettled. "A detective from the Nashville Police Department was just in yesterday gathering a few of the security guards' names. Now you are here about a murder in Hendersonville. Our security guards are really popular these days – and not in a good way."

"Sounds like," Sherri agreed, forcing a smile. "Do you have some way of trackin' one of them down for me?"

"I can sure try," Adrianna volunteered. Without hesitation, she reached to pick up her phone and punched in an extension. "Hang on," she said to the person on the other end of the connection. Hitting the hold button on her phone, she left the receiver between her chin and shoulder blade. Directing her attention back to Sherri, she asked, "What's the name of the security guard you are tryin' to locate?"

"Um…Debbie Gray," Sherri indicated. She leaned on the granite counter, waited, and listened to Adrianna talking to an unknown person on the phone.

"I have a Detective Ball here from the Hendersonville PD. She is lookin' for Debbie Gray. Is she down in the security console or is she somewhere else?" Adrianna asked.

There was a pause and then Sherri heard Adrianna say, "She *is* down in the security console. Okay…great! Can you send her to the lobby of the Administrative Office's Building? I'll send Detective Ball there to meet her. Just tell her Detective Ball will meet her by the front door. Okay… thanks," she said and hung up the phone. Directing her attention back to Sherri, Adrianna told her, "Debbie Gray will meet you by the front door in the lobby. Do I get some sort of reward if you guys catch this killer, since I've helped out detectives twice now?" she asked, a hopeful smirk appearing on her face.

"I don't know about a reward," Sherri replied. "But you do have my heartfelt thanks," she said, offering her hand.

Adrianna reached out and shook Sherri's hand. "I was only kidding about the reward anyway," she said. "I'm glad to help you guys. The sooner this killer is caught, the sooner I will feel safe again."

"That's what we're here for…to make citizens feel safe," Sherri said with a reassuring grin. "Thanks again for your help," she said and turned to go.

Adrianna's phone rang, and she reached to pick it up. Sherri hurried from the office, heading once more to the elevators and to her meeting with Debbie. She was both nervous and excited.

* * * *

Sherri took the elevator back to the lobby. There were several chairs sitting by the wall, across from the security guard, right inside the front door. Sherri took a seat in one of these chairs and waited.

Several minutes later, the front door was pulled open by a plump, black-haired woman. Sherri recognized this woman at once as Debbie Gray from the photograph Scott had shown her. The woman's arms were crossed and her lips were tight, as she gave Sherri a harsh stare. *I need to be careful. I need to put Debbie's mind at ease. I can't have her thinking the police are after her*, Sherri schemed.

Standing, and plastering on a huge, fake smile, Sherri thrust out her hand toward this stranger. "Debbie Gray?" she asked.

"Yes...I'm Debbie," she answered.

She uncrossed her arms and took Sherri's hand to shake it. But Debbie's grasp was very light and unconvincing. She was obviously wary of Sherri and of her intentions for being at her workplace and requesting a meeting with her.

"Debbie, I'm Detective Sherri Ball from the Hendersonvill' PD," she told her as Debbie released her hand. "Is there a cafeteria we can go to and sit down and talk for a few moments?"

"What do we need to talk about?" Debbie questioned in a gruff voice. She crossed her arms again, and a deep frown encased her mouth.

"I basically need your help," Sherri began to explain. "I'll be questionin' all of the security guards who were on duty the night Robert Oaks was murdered..."

"I already talked to the cops the night Robert Oaks died," Debbie interrupted her saying. "They found shoeprints from the murderer, and the prints from my shoes did not match. So what does a Hendersonville detective need with me?"

"We had a very similar murder in Hendersonvill' almost a month ago," Sherri explained.

Jack Jordan, Debbie mused. *Are they closing in on me for his murder and Robert Oaks?* "And? What's a murder in Hendersonville got to do with me?" Debbie questioned, staring Sherri down.

"We think our murder ties to the one in Nashville, but we still have no leads. I'm hopin' if I question each of you guys that one of you might have seen somethin' or heard somethin' that might give us a lead. I'd very much appreciate your time. I know you would like to help us get a killer off the street. Your job is to protect...much the same as mine," Sherri cleverly reminded with an encouraging grin. "So what do you say…can we go someplace and talk? I promise not to tie up much of your time. I'll even buy you a soft drink."

"I really don't have much time to spare," Debbie replied, softening her stance a bit. She dropped her arms to her sides. She seemed to be letting down her guard. "We can go to the lounge and sit down for a few, but I can tell you right now that you are really wasting your time with me. Of all four security guards involved that night, I had the least contact with Robert Oaks or his murder site. Any reason in particular that you picked me first?"

"Actually…" Sherri said with a chuckle. "I have to meet with Nashville detectives in about a half hour…actually less now…" she relayed, glancing at her watch. "I thought I'd start with the security guard who probably has the least to say. And as you've already indicated…that would be you. But I still want to get your observations. And your observations could well be different than any of the other security guards because you are the only woman," Sherri continued to fabricate. "So which way is the lounge? Can we be on the way there, and get this show on the road?" Sherri hopped around as if she was anxious now.

Debbie stepped around her. "I'll take you to the lounge," she said, heading toward the elevators. "The sooner we get this over with the better. And hopefully, this will be the last time I'll have to talk to the cops about this."

"Oh…I'm sure it will be," Sherri tried to assure her. *Hopefully, the next time the cops come to see you it will be with an arrest warrant*, she thought.

An empty elevator car arrived and they stepped aboard. They were joined by a few other ladies. The elevator doors closed and the elevator lifted. Sherri's insides danced as the elevator carried all aboard to their destinations and allowed Sherri a crucial chance to get a DNA sample from Debbie Gray.

Chapter 20

Moving On

The sun glistened on Sherri's wide smile as she walked out of the Gaylord's administrative offices. As she raced along the sidewalk, passing the rest of the Gaylord Entertainment Center, she glanced at the impressive glass cone and looming spire on top of the Gaylord. In mimicking an old radio station antenna, it gave the building a touch of history, yet still added a unique, eye-catching look.

Cars and busses whizzed by on the street beside her – Broadway. The air whipped and tangled Sherri's hair, but she did not care. The sun caressed her face and body, warming the breeze and escalating Sherri's good mood even more.

She stepped forward onto the crosswalk with others in front, to the side, and in back of her. She could hear their voices, but Sherri paid no heed to the conversations going on all about her. Her mind was preoccupied by her successful meeting with Debbie Gray and her upcoming reunion with Scott. Sherri could not wait to share her happy news with him. Her gait was so lively that she almost skipped along the city sidewalk, darting past others who walked slower.

Sherri also rushed past towering, sidewalk-shading buildings. The honkytonks, souvenir stores, and restaurants were all a blur. Sherri's nose and stomach were the only parts of her paying attention to her surroundings. Her stomach reacted to her sense of smell, growling, as it was enticed by some of the aromas emitting from the eateries.

Sherri darted down a side street. Looking both ways and noting a welcome gap in traffic, she dashed across the street and into a public parking lot. As her legs sped toward Scott's van, she heard the automatic lock click. Sherri thrust open the passenger door, hopped inside, shut the door, and pressed down on the lock button.

"You certainly look happy," Scott commented, observing her dazzling smile. He returned one of his own.

"You betcha, I am!" Sherri exclaimed. She pulled her purse from her shoulder, sat it in her lap, and reached inside to pull forth a sealed plastic bag. Inside the bag was a straw. Holding the bag in front of Scott's face, swinging it back and forth, and laughing triumphantly, she said, "Ready-made DNA at my fingertips."

"Hot damn! Good Job!" Scott praised with a pleased chuckle. Then he asked in a more somber voice, "Did Debbie Gray seem suspicious of you at all?"

"At first…yes," Sherri admitted, placing the bag safely inside her purse and laying her purse on the floor at her feet. Sitting up and looking Scott in the eye, she elaborated, "But I managed to bullshit enough to set her mind at ease. So that garnered me a sit down in the employee lounge with her. And to sweeten the pot, I had Debbie round up one of the other security guards who were on duty the night of Robert Oaks' death. When she left the room, I stole her straw from the drink I bought her. I replaced it with a fresh straw. I have a meetin' with a third security guard set for tomorrow. I'll be sure and meet with the other one as well just for good measure."

"Sherri, you are extraordinary!" Scott praised.

He slid across the seat and engulfed her in a grateful hug. He had only intended for it to be a congratulatory hug. But as he drew back and looked into Sherri's chocolate, caring eyes, and fingered her unusually disheveled hair, Scott's desire got the best of him. He found himself drawing Sherri into a pursuing kiss.

Sherri did not push him away. Quite the opposite, she threw her arms around Scott's neck and pulled herself in as close as she could get. They pleasured one another with sucking lips and probing tongues for several, heated moments.

"Sc...Scott," Sherri finally uttered in a breathy voice, pushing back from him.

"Yeah," he responded, his wanting eyes burning into hers. He still held Sherri and did not wish to let her go.

"We...uh...we're supposed to be workin' here," Sherri reminded him. Her whole body trembled as her weak wrists pushed out of his arms. She scooted against the door. "We need to get this DNA to the crime lab, Scott. Catchin' Debbie Gray needs to be our primary focus." She was sounding more logical the more she talked. Only Sherri's gleaming, passion-filled eyes betrayed her true desires.

Scott was reluctant to scoot back to his side of the van, but he realized what Sherri said was true. The sooner they got the DNA to the crime lab, the sooner they would have the results back on the testing, and the sooner Jeanette Peterson could be put away once and for all. With these thoughts, Scott's head cleared.

"Alright," he agreed with a short laugh, sliding back over behind the steering wheel. "But...how about we get together again after you get off work? What time do you get off duty this evening?"

"Um...I pick up my daughter tonight after I get off work, and I have her until Sunday evenin'. My ex-husband and I have joint custody. I have Angela three or four days, and then he has her the next three or four, and so on. And he works around my schedule," Sherri explained. She was somewhat relieved she would have Angela. She needed a reprieve from Scott for a few days.

"Angela..." Scott repeated. "That's a pretty name. That's the first time you've actually mentioned your daughter's name. And...just for the record...I think it's great that your ex works around your schedule, but I think it would have been far better if he had worked harder on your marriage. You're a great lady, Sherri. I can't imagine any man cheating and walking away from a relationship with you."

Scott's words and his appreciative gaze touched Sherri's heart. She looked away out the windshield, tapped her hand on the dash, and replied, "Thanks." Then glancing back at Scott, she reminded him, "We should be goin'."

She doesn't want to talk about her marriage or her ex, Scott concluded. He did not want to make Sherri feel uncomfortable or rain on her parade of success. "Yeah," he responded, sticking his key in the ignition and starting the engine.

He would take her back to the station for now and let her process the evidence she had gathered. But Scott was not through pursuing a relationship other than business with Sherri. He had never expected to feel this close to a woman again after Debbie died. He was not about to let Sherri slip away.

Tuning the radio to Sherri's favorite country station, Scott shifted the van into drive and headed out, eager to get her back to the station and for Sherri to start processing Debbie Gray's DNA sample. *Enjoy your freedom while you still have it, Jeanette*, he contemplated with relish. *Because we are closing in on you.* A smile came to Scott's face, and he stepped down harder on the accelerator.

Chapter 21

Strange Session

Friday afternoon, Debbie sat in the waiting area at Dr. Cleaver's – five chairs by the wall across from his secretary's desk. Dr. Cleaver did not have a separate waiting room, because rarely did a patient have to wait on him. He was usually pretty prompt about taking patients on time.

Debbie alternated between thumbing through a magazine and watching Marissa work at her desk. Marissa was a young, fair-skinned, wide-eyed, innocent-looking young woman. Debbie guessed she must be Irish because of her auburn hair and vivid blue eyes.

Busy typing something into her PC, Marissa paid Debbie no heed. Debbie was both curious and nervous about today's session with Dr. Cleaver. She feared what could happen if she unleashed her full anger on Wally. *Will he really have a way to control it? If not, how do I keep from hurting...or even killing...him?* Debbie could not help but wonder.

"Marissa," Debbie heard the secretary's intercom bellow.

Marissa pushed a button and replied, "Yes, Dr. Cleaver."

"Send Debbie Gray in," Wally directed.

"Okay," his secretary agreed. Then releasing the intercom button, Marissa turned toward Debbie. Smiling, she said, "Debbie, the doctor will see you now. Go right in."

Debbie stood and laid her magazine in the seat of her now vacant chair. She directed her legs toward Dr. Cleaver's closed office door. Grabbing the doorknob, she turned it, and pushed open the door.

Debbie was surprised to find Dr. Cleaver sitting in the chair in front of his desk – the one she usually occupied. His top button was undone; his tie was loosened; and he was sock-footed. And something else was amiss; the office was bright. Debbie noted the mini-blinds were cranked wide open, allowing sunshine to spill all across the room.

"Hello, Debbie," Dr. Cleaver addressed with an idiotic smile spread ear to ear.

"Hi, Wally," she replied, sounding unsure as she closed the door.

Debbie stood just inside the door, staring at him, not sure where she should go. She looked – and felt – out of place. *If Dr. Cleaver's intention, with his chair-switching stunt, odd appearance, and sun-drenched office, is to throw me off balance, he's accomplished that*, Debbie decided.

"You look uncomfortable, Debbie," Wally commented. "Is something the matter?"

"I…uh…. You're in my chair," Debbie pointed out, sounding exasperated and feeling foolish. *Maybe he's trying to make me feel awkward in hopes I'll get angry,* she tried to reason.

"Does that bother you?" he asked, crossing his hands at his waist and pointing his index fingers out at her.

"Well…you said I look uncomfortable. What do you think?" Debbie asked in a sassy voice. She crossed her arms across her chest.

"I'm supposed to be the one asking the questions here, Debbie," Dr. Cleaver reminded her, swiveling his chair back and forth. "And this is *my* office, so I can sit in any damn chair I please. Have you got a problem with that?"

He's being adversarial, Debbie noted. "Obviously I do," she replied. *Let's see how he likes a dose of his own medicine*, she concluded.

Debbie proceeded to head behind Dr. Cleaver's desk and took a seat in *his* chair. Leaning back, she dared to kick his discarded shoes. She was surprised when she found them heavy. She looked down at them and saw that they were uniform type shoes, not his typical shiny dress shoes.

Ignoring his odd shoes, Debbie looked up at Dr. Cleaver with her arms still crossed, and challenged, "So how do you like me being in *your* chair?"

"You know what? You're a real smartass!" Dr. Cleaver declared.

Springing out of his chair, he slammed his palms down in the middle of his desk. Debbie jumped at his sudden movement and the banging of his hands. Her arms flailed apart and she leaned back in the chair. Dr. Cleaver dared to bend in toward Debbie. Like a mad, snarling dog, he bared his teeth and barked, "Get your ass out of my chair and from behind my desk!"

Wally's glowering eyes burned a hole through her. Debbie could almost swear that Dr. Cleaver was genuinely angry. *And genuinely crazy!* "Is this how you think my father acted, Wally?" she asked, trying to make sense of it all.

Pushing her chair back and standing, Debbie made her way around the side of his desk, putting more of a barrier between the two of them again. She thought Dr. Cleaver would surely go behind his desk now. But instead, he stood right where he was, glaring at her. Debbie, once again, was unsure where she should go.

"What the hell does your father have to do with anything?" Wally shocked her by asking.

If Wally was putting on an act, it was highly believable to Debbie. She kept her position to the side of his desk. "You said we were going to role-play in this session. You're supposed to pretend to be my mother...or father...and I'm supposed to say to you what I would have liked to say to them," she reminded him, studying him with narrowed, questioning eyes.

"I can't believe people actually buy into that silly shit," Dr. Cleaver commented, laughing and shaking his head. Walking over to the sofa, he took a sprawling seat. "So did your daddy spank you, Debbie?" he asked in a whiny, condescending voice. "If you'd like, I can turn you over my knee. Now, *that* might be fun."

"Look, Wally, this session isn't making any sense to me," Debbie confided. She walked across the room, cranked the mini-blinds to their usual position – closed – and sat down in one of the chairs at the table. She needed to keep some distance between her and this lunatic that was supposed to be her doctor. "My dad wasn't sexually abusive if that's what you're trying to get at. I'm not angry at him because of anything like that. I'm angry with my parents because they forced me to be something…or someone…I was not," she reiterated. She reached to grab a glass and poured herself some iced water from the pitcher on the table in front of her.

"Ohhh!" Wally wailed. Then placing his index finger on his lips and quivering them, he added, "Pooor, pooor baby! I feel so sorry for you. Your mommy and daddy made you be someone you weren't. What a crock of shit! Why don't you just grow up and get over it?! I don't know if I can sit here and listen to all this crap! Being a head doctor is highly overrated. No wonder it pays so well."

"Is this your way of trying to make me angry, Wally?" Debbie asked, rolling her glass in her hands. "I'm not sure what role you are trying to play…but…this is just bizarre," she told him, studying him with perplexed eyes. Debbie was not angry; she was merely confused.

"You think *I'm* bizarre? This comes from Ms…I want you to pretend to be my daddy," he addressed her, mocking her more. "Okay…I'll bite. What exactly did you want to say to your mom and dad? This could be good for shits and giggles. Go ahead. Get it over with. The sooner the better. Then we can end this bullshit session. What's the point of all this exactly, anyway?"

"The point, according to you, is that it is supposed to be a way for me to get all my anger out. Then I won't fantasize about killing people," Debbie stated, still eyeballing him peculiarly.

"Fantasize about killing people...or actually kill them?" Wally dared to ask. He had straightened up on the sofa and his face had become serious.

"What are you asking me, Wally?" Debbie questioned, her face scrunched up in bewilderment. This session got stranger and stranger by the minute.

"I'm not asking you anything....Debbie....*Debbie*... that's your name, right?" he asked, rubbing his hands together and slightly smiling.

First that cop comes and talks to me yesterday. Now...Wally is acting really weird...and it sounds as if he is accusing me of murder. Could someone be on to something? Debbie wondered, beginning to get spooked.

She sat her glass down on the table and stood. "Look, Wally, this session isn't really working today. I think we need to call it quits."

"Why do you look so rattled all the sudden, J.... Uh...Debbie?" Wally asked. His smile had widened. He was showing his teeth now.

What name did he almost call me? Debbie thought with added alarm. She had stopped dead in her tracks, and she was trying not to fidget with her hands. "I'm not rattled, Wally," she argued. "I've just had enough of this farce. I don't intend to pay for today's session."

"I think you have a lot more to be concerned about than paying for some stupid psychiatric session, Debbie," Dr. Cleaver pointed out, an evil glint to his eyes. "How about paying for the murders you've committed?"

"What the hell are you talking about, Wally?" Debbie asked, placing her trembling hands on her hips to stabilize them. *He can't possibly* really *know anything. This must be a game he's playing. But why?* she wondered. *Could the cops be on to something? Could they have come to Wally? Could he be working with them?* Her mind raced. *I need to get out of here!*

"This session is over, Wally. You are the one who needs psychiatric help," Debbie declared, as she started for the door.

"Bye, Debbie. I'll be seeing you around," he proclaimed with a wicked chuckle, as she opened the door and practically ran out, slamming the door behind her. "Run, Jeanette! You can run, but you can't hide!" he declared, throwing himself back on the couch in an insane fit of laughter.

The session had ended, and Dr. Cleaver had thrown all his cards on the table. He did not care. He was tired of playing games. He was in control now, and that was where he intended to stay. Jeanette – or Debbie Gray as he was now known – was his ticket to fun, and he fully planned to continue to have some fun.

Wally got up from the couch, walked over behind his desk, and slipped on his shoes. It was a beautiful day outside, and he needed a breath of free air. Even though this session had ended on a high note, the first part of it had drained him. Wally headed toward the door, eager to get away from the office for awhile and to relish the fear of God he had put into Debbie Gray. *Knowledge and power are fun*, he concluded, as he skipped out of his office, telling Marissa he would be back in about an hour, in plenty of time for his next appointment.

Chapter 22

The Teacher

Almost a month later, Sherri was still awaiting the results of DNA testing on the straw she had stolen from Debbie Gray. She was relieved Debbie had not killed again. Sherri was sitting in her office, working at her desk, when her ringing phone demanded attention. She reached to raise the receiver. "Sergeant Ball," she answered.

"Hello, Sergeant," a familiar voice replied back. "I need a moment of your time this afternoon. Could you please meet me here at police headquarters?"

"Of course I can, Geoffrey," Sherri assured him with lighthearted inflection in her voice. She was surprised by his serious tone and the way he had addressed her. He usually called her by her first name and was more jovial when talking to her. "When did you want to meet with me? Does this have anything to do with the Robert Oaks homicide? Has there been a break in the case?" she asked with hopefulness.

"I'd like to meet with you ASAP," the lieutenant replied, an air of urgency in his voice. "And this has to do with another homicide that just occurred day before yesterday," he revealed.

"Same MO?" she clarified, pushing back her desk chair and standing.

"Same MO," he gruffly confirmed. "So how soon can you get here?"

"I'll be there ASAP," she pledged, sounding eager.

"Okay. I'll see you in a few," Geoffrey curtly responded.

They ended their call then. Sherri was anxious to hear the details of this new case. *Damn! Debbie Gray has struck again*, she thought with aggravation and remorse. *I need to press the lab for results on the DNA sample I sent them.*

"Newton," she called her partner. When he turned to look at her, Sherri revealed, "I've got to run over to the Nashville PD. Hold down the fort while I'm gone. I don't know how long I'll be there. There's been another homicide. Same MO as the Jack Jordan murder here in Hendersonville."

"Man, we really have a serial killer runnin' around, don't we?" he commented, looking concerned.

"Looks that way," Sherri agreed, nodding her head.

She pulled open a lower desk drawer and snatched up her purse. Turning, she made haste toward the door leading out of the office area. The sooner she got to the Nashville PD, the better. And the sooner she got back her DNA results from the straw she had snatched from Debbie Gray, even better. Sherri was eager to make an arrest in this case. The killings needed to stop.

* * * *

When Sherri arrived at the Metropolitan Nashville Police Department, Geoff was waiting for her in the lobby by the information booth. Today, there were no flirty, happy greetings for Sherri from Lieutenant Gregory. Geoff never even cracked a smile. He just marched off with Sherri trailing him, leading her to his office.

Wonder what he's got in his crawl, Sherri pondered, noting Geoff's rigid body language. *He almost looks like he's mad about something.*

He stopped at the door to his office and let Sherri pass. She walked into Geoff's small office, slid back the single chair, and had a seat, surveying her surroundings. A small wooden desk sat in front of her. A computer monitor took up a good portion of it, and what was left of the top was covered by stacks and stacks of paper. Geoffrey's office mirrored the control freak he was. Heaven forbid he would have a secretary file any of the items piled high on his desk.

Sherri heard the door close, and she watched as Geoffrey walked around his desk and also had a seat. Tapping his fingertips together and locking his cold gray eyes with Sherri's warm brown ones, he finally spoke, saying, "A female preschool teacher from Tiny Tykes Academy is our latest victim. She was found behind the school yesterday morning. Death was, of course, a mortal wound to the carotid. She was handcuffed and knifed in the vaginal area, postmortem."

"As you already said…same MO as our other murders," Sherri stated. "So why did you ask me to come to your office?" she wasted no time inquiring, squirming in her seat. With the office door closed, the small, cluttered space was making Sherri a bit claustrophobic. Geoffrey could have easily told me what he just did over the phone. He obviously has another reason for my requested visit, Sherri concluded, waiting with impatience for his reply.

Lieutenant Gregory sat back in his chair and placed his foot on top of his other leg, crossing his legs. Tapping on his elevated thigh and pursing his lips, he finally revealed, "One of the parking lot cameras at Tiny Tykes captured images of a van with out-of-state plates parking by the school on several occasions. No children were dropped off from this van, and no one got out. They just parked. We ran the plates, and guess who the van belongs to?"

"Oh my God!" Sherri exclaimed, her eyes widening and her mouth dropping open. She placed her hand over her gaping mouth as she guessed it must have been Scott's van on the video. "She killed her own daughter's daycare teacher," she mumbled, speaking her stunned thoughts aloud.

"Who killed their daughter's daycare teacher?" Geoffrey asked, making out what Sherri had just uttered. "What are you involved in, Sherri?" he questioned, rapping his knuckles on his bottom lip. "Or maybe I should ask *who* you are involved *with*?"

"I'm not sure I like the insinuation of your last question, Geoffrey," Sherri told him, her lips taut. She linked her hands and tapped her index fingers. "My personal life is none of your business," she tartly stated.

"It is if it interferes with a serial homicide investigation," he argued, grabbing the end of his shoe and squeezing the toe. "I think you have been working with Scott Arnold on the Robert Oaks homicide…which frankly, Sherri, it's not your case to work…."

"You are absolutely right, Geoffrey," Sherri agreed, nodding her head. But there was a displeased smirk on her face. "And normally, I would have had absolutely nothin' to do with a Nashville homicide case. But this one ties directly into a grisly homicide in Hendersonville. That opens the door to me…."

"It opens the door for *you* to work with *Nashville* investigators on the case. It certainly does *not* open the door for you to work with a *PI*….and yes, I do know Scott Arnold is a PI now, even though you both misrepresented him as a detective from LMPD when I initially met him. No wonder he was dressed like a street person when we met. No respectable homicide detective would have looked like he did," Geoffrey grumbled, disapproval written all over his face. He pulled on his elevated leg with both hands and swiveled his chair.

"Look, Geoffrey, you need to stop bein' so hard-nosed about separatin' police jurisdictions and detectives from private investigators. Scott has been a big help on this case. In fact, his lead may soon have the cases bustin' wide open. Our main initiative – all of us – needs to be solvin' these cases and bringin' a killer to justice," Sherri argued, crossing her arms.

"And how do you know that this killer is not Scott Arnold?" Geoff shocked her by suggesting.

"What?" Sherri spit out with a disbelieving laugh, shaking her head. "How'd you come by that one, Geoff?" She shortened his name, irritated with him.

"Well, let's look at the facts," Lieutenant Gregory suggested, tapping on his shoe. "Scott Arnold quit his job as a homicide detective in Louisville, KY. The string of serial killings ceased after he left the force. One of the victims was his girlfriend; and guess who police found at the murder site, kneeling in her blood? Now, he shows up in Nashville, and there have been three murders with the exact MO's of the unsolved Louisville murders. And his van was caught casing the schoolhouse of our latest victim. He sounds like a worthy suspect to me. You need to stop letting your libido cloud your judgment, Sherri," Geoff chastised, leaning back in his chair and folding his hands at his waist.

"I already warned you about bringin' my personal life into this," Sherri protested through gritted teeth. She crossed her arms even tighter and leaned back in her chair. "Whatever is…or isn't…between Scott and I is none of your business. And it has nothin' to do with the way I'm investigatin' these homicides. I think it's your judgment that's bein' clouded here…clouded by jealousy. You've flirted with me since before I was divorced…even more so since the divorce. Now, you see Scott gainin' ground and you can't stand it."

"So *is* Scott gaining ground?" Geoffrey had the nerve to ask. He had a smug expression on his face, as if to say 'told you so'.

"I won't dignify that with an answer," Sherri replied, exhaling in frustration. "The only thing I will say is that your accusations against Scott have no merit. Scott has evidence to back up his theories. There was DNA found at two of the Louisvill' homicides, and it didn't belong to Scott. And the shoeprints found at our Hendersonvill' murder and your Nashvill' one sure couldn't belong to Scott. He's a tall guy with big feet – a lot bigger than eight…eight and a half. So how do you explain these facts, Geoffrey?" she challenged, her blazing eyes boring into him.

"So what was Scott's reason for casing the daycare where our latest victim was found?" Geoff asked, not willing to concede he might be mistaken about Scott.

Sherri silently eyeballed Geoff for a few moments. Then she uncrossed her arms, pushed up on the arms of the chair, and stood. "You know what, Geoffrey, you're right," he was surprised to hear Sherri reveal. But then she clarified. "I should not have gotten involved in investigatin' your Nashvill' homicide. I need to stick to workin' on the Hendersonvill' one. And whoever I choose to work with on that case is really none of your business. And whatever methods we use is none of your business either. I think we are done here today."

"Sherri, this latest homicide occurred in Nashville again. I could have Scott Arnold pulled in for questioning," he threatened, uncrossing his legs and leaning forward in his chair.

"You do what you need to do, Geoffrey," Sherri said, starring him down. "And I'll do what I need to do," she promised.

Standing up straight and trying to exude confidence, Sherri turned her back on Lieutenant Gregory and walked the few steps to his door. She did not hesitate to jerk it open. Without looking back, she made quick strides out the door, pulling it closed behind her. She stopped just shy of slamming it.

I need to get in touch with Scott, she quickly ascertained. *He needs to know what Geoffrey is up to. But first, I need to make sure a rush is put on that DNA testing. I need to have concrete proof of our case. Then Lieutenant Gregory can go straight to hell!*

Sherri walked out into the hall and raced toward the exit door. When she reached the lobby, she sidestepped several people, veering off to the other side of the information booth. Whipping out her cell phone, Sherri dialed Scott's cell number. She placed the phone to her ear and started walking toward the exit doors.

Scott answered on the third ring. "Hello, beautiful, how are you?" he answered, spotting Sherri's name on his caller ID.

"Scott, this isn't a social call," Sherri cautioned, her voice dead serious. She was outside now.

"What's up?" he asked, also turning serious.

"Where are you? Are you in Kentucky or Tennessee?" she questioned. She was in the parking lot, heading for her car. The summer, afternoon sun, beating down on the black asphalt, cooked the bottoms of Sherri's flat pumps. It made her hurry all the more toward her car.

"I'm in Kentucky, why?" Scott asked. "Do you need me to come to Tennessee?"

"No," she replied, sounding cagey. "I'm goin' to come to Kentucky."

"You are coming *here*?" Scott questioned, sounding even more concerned. "What's up, Sherri?"

"I'll explain it all to you when we talk face to face," she assured him. "For now, I'm headin' back to the station. I have some things I need to take care of before I leave." *I'm going to get a rush put on that DNA testing.* "I'll call you from the station to get your address."

Scott heard a slam and a chiming. He guessed Sherri had just gotten in her car and turned the ignition key. He wanted to ask her why she could not get his address from him now, but he sensed she did not want to take it over the cell phone. *Something's up.* Of that, he was certain.

"I'll talk to you in a little bit," Sherri told him. She had started the car and turned the air conditioning on high. Right now, it blew hot air.

"Okay. I'll be awaiting your call," Scott replied. *Anxiously*, he knew.

Sherri backed her car up, put it in drive, and headed out of the parking lot. Turning onto the street, she headed toward the expressway and her route back to the Hendersonville Police

Department. "Bye. I'll see you soon," she said into her cell phone.

"Bye," Scott replied.

Taking the phone away from his ear, Scott saw Sherri's number flashing on his phone, signaling their call had ended. He closed his phone and attempted to concentrate on the task at hand. Scott was working another insurance fraud case and doing surveillance on the home of the alleged scammer.

Even if Sherri left Nashville at that very moment, she would not be in Louisville for over two hours, so he knew he might as well continue to work. However, it was extremely hard for Scott to concentrate. His mind was engrossed by Sherri and whatever had her so upset that she needed to drive to Louisville to talk to him. He would be glad – in more ways than one – when he could see and talk with her.

Scott had not physically seen Sherri in almost a month. He *had* talked to her on the phone on several occasions. On each occasion, he had tried to persuade Sherri to go out on a date with him. During their last call, her resolve not to date him had seemed to be waning considerably. Scott had thought that might be what she was calling about today. But now he knew it was something far more serious. Her next call could not come soon enough for him, and neither could Sherri's all-important visit to his Louisville, Kentucky home.

Chapter 23

Connections

Sherri arrived at Scott's house – a small Cape Cod in Pleasure Ridge Park, a district in the south end of Louisville – about 8:45 p.m. Louisville time. Scott's heart rate elevated at the sight of her. As usual, she looked extraordinary. Sherri was dressed in an attractive royal blue pantsuit, with the jacket fitted at her shapely waist, and her black hair shone in the setting sun.

Scott watched through his picture window as Sherri sauntered up his front walk. He did not wait for her to knock or ring the bell. Instead, as she climbed the front porch steps, he thrust open both the front and the storm door. Startled by Scott's abrupt appearance, Sherri shuddered and stopped dead in her tracks at the edge of the porch.

"Sorry! I didn't mean to scare you," he said, stepping out and allowing the storm door to softly close at his back. "How was your drive? Have you eaten dinner yet?" he fired questions at her. He was so excited to see Sherri, he felt like a kid on Christmas day .

Sherri gave him a smile, noting his casual style – tan cargo shorts, a University of Louisville T-shirt, and athletic shoes without socks. "Um…the drive was fine. As to dinner, I went through the drive-through at McDonalds. Not the most nutritious meal in the world…but fillin'," she responded to his questions.

Sherri was trying to ignore Scott's hairy legs. It was the first time she had ever seen Scott's legs. He had always worn jeans or dress slacks the other times she had seen him.

The plentiful dark hair on Scott's legs had her unchastely wondering if his chest was as hairy.

"Well, welcome to my home, Sherri," Scott said with a beaming smile. He turned and pulled the storm door open. Then leaning against it, he motioned for Sherri to pass.

As expected, Sherri entered the house. Scott caught her enticing scent as she passed. His heartbeat sped up even more. Sherri took a second to appraise her surroundings. A small living room with exposed hardwood floors, it still contained a leather sofa and club chair, a glass-topped coffee and side tables, and some lamps.

Sherri was not really concerned with what Scott's house looked like. She was there to see him. When she turned, she found that Scott had also entered the house. He had shut the front door and was standing against it, staring at her.

"What?" Sherri asked, her brow puckering.

"I...what I'd really like to do right now is close the distance between us, take you in my arms, and kiss you until we're both oxygen deprived," he truthfully confessed, a hoarse edge to his voice.

"See why I've kept my distance from you," Sherri stated, shaking her index finger at him. But her radiant smile betrayed her amusement. Truth be known, part of her wanted to tell Scott to close that distance. "We need to keep it all business for now, Scott. I really need to talk to you," Sherri told him, sounding much too serious. Her smile disappeared.

"Okay," he reluctantly agreed. "Have a seat. I straightened up a little before you came, so there is plenty of seating to choose from. Just don't open any of the closets," he warned with a snicker. As he watched Sherri step over to the couch and sit down, Scott asked, "Can I get you something to drink? I have Budweiser, coke, coffee or water."

"You know what? A beer sounds pretty darn good right now," Sherri surprised him by saying, sounding flustered.

"Okay...Bud it is then," Scott agreed. "Do you drink it out of the bottle, or would you like it in a glass?"

"In a glass, please," she said, flashing him a grateful smile.

"Okay. Comin' right up," he replied, and headed through the living room and off to the kitchen.

Sherri could hear Scott rattling around in the kitchen. As she waited for him to return, she looked out the picture window directly across from her. A man across the street was mowing his lawn.

Scott appeared a few moments later with a bottle of Budweiser for himself and a glass full of beer for Sherri. He handed her the glass, took a seat on the sofa, and reached to switch on the lamp beside him. A click brought a warm glow to the room, eliminating shadows brought about by the setting sun.

"What has you so worked up that you had to drive to Louisville to talk with me?" Scott asked, taking a drink of his beer. "Not that I mind you being here," he added with an easy grin.

Sherri raised her glass and took a drink before she said, "There was another murder in Nashvill' two days ago, Scott."

"Crap!" he swore, taking a larger swig from his bottle. "Who this time?"

"I'd say, 'You won't believe it', but I know you will," Sherri stated, taking another drink from her glass. Rolling it between the palms of her hands, she revealed, "It was the preschool teacher from Tiny Tykes Academy."

"Unbelievable!" Scott exclaimed, drinking still more beer. "Although...as you said...it's not that hard for me to believe. After all, Jeanette already killed both of Susanna's parents, so what's the big deal about killing a meager preschool teacher?"

"Yeah. I guess that's true," Sherri agreed, her mouth contorting with disapproval.

"I'm sorry to hear that Jeanette has killed again. But that is not what has you driving from Nashville. We could have covered this in a phone conversation. So what's the real reason for your visit, Sherri?" Scott questioned, finishing off the last of his beer and sitting the empty bottle on the table in front of him.

Sherri took another hearty sampling from her glass. Then making direct eye contact with Scott, she said, "Geoffrey summoned me to the Nashvill' PD today...."

"Uh-oh! Why don't I like the sound of this?" Scott asked, rubbing the side of his face. It was clean-shaven. He had combed his hair and shaved just before Sherri had arrived. "Should I go and get myself another beer? Would you like another?" he inquired, noticing her glass was almost empty.

"No. I'm fine," she answered. "Go get yourself another if you like."

"Nah. I'm more interested in staying right here and hearing what you have to say," Scott probed. He was literally hanging on the edge of his seat.

"Your van was caught on one of the preschool's parkin' lot surveillance cameras. Your Kentucky plates drew attention," Sherri shared. She finished off her own drink and sat her glass beside Scott's bottle.

"And of course, Geoffrey tracked the plates back to me. Does he know we are working together now?" he asked. Sliding a leg up on the couch and tossing his arm along the top, he turned more toward Sherri.

"*Oh*...yeah!" Sherri confirmed, nodding her head. "Not only that but...are you ready for this?"

"Bring it on," Scott invited, holding a hand out and curling his fingers in toward himself.

"Geoffrey tried to finger you as a suspect," she confessed, rolling her eyes and shaking her head.

"Oh, that's a good one!" Scott declared, scratching his chin and laughing at the absurdity. "And what evidence...other than my van being seen at the murder scene...does he think he has on me? Can you tell me that?"

"He has absolutely nothin', Scott," she declared. "Geoffrey's on the warpath because he thinks the two of us are romantically involved, and he can't stand it. He even came off with some crap about you bein' found at your girlfriend's murder site kneelin' in her blood. How crazy is that?" Sherri questioned with a disbelieving giggle, shaking her head.

"Sounds like good ol' Geoff has really done his homework," Scott replied, his brow furrowing and his lips tightly puckering.

"Is the story about your girlfriend…it isn't true, is it?" Sherri inquired, looking concerned for the first time.

"Oh…it's true alright," Scott confirmed, pinching his bottom lip. "But Geoffrey didn't tell the whole story. I was cleared of any wrongdoing by the Public Integrity Unit," he revealed. Then he continued, his eyes taking on a faraway look. "I was the first one to find Debbie. It's a lot different finding someone you love murdered. I wanted her to be alive so bad that I bent down over her. When I did, I slipped and fell…right over the top of her. Shively police showed up just at that moment. I still consider that to be the worst day of my life. First, I find the love of my life dead, and then through my clumsiness, I disrupt the crime scene. Next time you see Geoff, thank him for making me relive that day…yet again," Scott uttered, looking pained. "I think I will have another beer after all," he said, standing. "Can I get you another one?"

"Sure," Sherri agreed. Another beer might help to take the edge off. She felt terrible that she had brought up this accusation and caused Scott pain over Debbie's death once more. Sherri had never dreamed that this crazy rambling by Geoffrey could be true. *Or at least partially true.*

Scott returned a few minutes later with two more beers. Sherri took a moment to pour hers into her glass. Scott was already drinking his. "Scott, I'm sorry I brought up the day of Debbie's murder," Sherri apologized. "I shouldn't have been so insensitive."

"You know…no matter how much time passes… Debbie's death still stabs at me like a knife. I should have been able to protect her," he declared, sitting and sucking down more brew. His eyes looked very sad.

Sherri took a drink from her glass. Then she reached to squeeze Scott's hand. "I know it's not the same, Scott, but my divorce felt like a death. It still tears at my heart. So I can definitely feel for you. What can I do to make this all better?"

Scott allowed his eyes to wander back to Sherri's. Her caring eyes touched his heart. He sat his bottle down on the table. Then he reached to take her glass from her and also sit it on the table.

Sliding over on the couch, he closed the distance between them. He reached with his hand and began to caress Sherri's silky, ivory cheek. "Neither one of us should have lost the one we loved," he commented. "But here we are. So where do we go from here? Do we let broken hearts ruin the rest of our lives? Or do we move forward?"

Scott's hand felt wonderful touching Sherri's cheek. She closed her eyes and allowed herself to enjoy his gentle touch for a few moments. She had a buzz, and it was not from the beer.

Opening her eyes, Sherri murmured in a quiet voice, "Scott."

"Hmm," he responded, fingering her lips. Sherri kissed his fingertips.

"You're right," she declared. Her eyes, gleaming with desire, were mirrors of Scott's.

"What am I right about?" he asked in a whisper, drawing in even closer. Sherri could feel his hot breath on her face.

"I don't want to let a broken heart ruin the rest of my life. I want to move forward," she told him, reaching to outline his lips with her finger.

"Anyone in particular you'd like to move forward with?" Scott questioned with a knowing chuckle, giving her lips a brush with his.

"*Oh*…yeah!" Sherri proclaimed with zest, tossing her arms around his neck and pulling their mouths together.

Sherri was done holding back. She cared a great deal about Scott, and she believed he felt the same way about her. They made a great team as investigators. Now, it was time to see if they made as great of a team otherwise.

Sherri continued to kiss Scott with reckless abandon. Right now, she wanted to live for the moment. And the moment called for passion. She would deny herself the pleasure no more.

Chapter 24

Panic

Debbie huffed and puffed as she stacked another box in the corner of her living room. Her move from Kentucky almost two years ago had been much easier. But then again, she had been twenty-five pounds lighter. *Once I move and get settled in my new home, I'll diet and lose some weight*, she planned.

Debbie took a seat on the couch, intent on taking a breather. She wiped some sweat from her brow. She was happy to realize that she had just about packed all she needed. She was following her plan – take only what she considered essential and what she believed might fit in the cargo van she intended to rent.

Debbie had been scheming, and working on, this move since her last – crazy – session with Dr. Cleaver. That episode, right on the heels of her suspicious chit-chat with the detective from Hendersonville, had Debbie itching to get out of the Nashville area. Now, she had the murder of Ms. Atkins, Susanna's preschool teacher, to add to her list of reasons to find a new home.

Debbie knew it would not be long before police came knocking on her door. She was linked in some way to all of the victims. Detectives would eventually connect the dots. And if they tied her into these Nashville murders, it was feasible that they might also discover that she was really Jeanette Peterson. Then she would not only be tried in court for the murders in Tennessee but in Kentucky as well. *Yes, it's well past time I found a new haunt*, she told herself again.

Debbie groaned as she placed her hands on the sofa cushion, to each side of herself, and pushed her chubby frame to a standing position. Her body was sore, and she was tired. She had been packing each night after she put Susanna to bed.

Her daughter was very smart and perceptive. She had noticed the boxes stacking up around the house. "Mommy, what are in the boxes?" Susanna had asked with an eager grin. Her daughter associated boxes with presents. Debbie guessed the little girl figured it must be nearing either Christmas or her birthday.

"They are for a *big* surprise," Debbie had told her.

"Are they for me?" Susanna had asked, pointing to herself and swinging her tiny body back and forth.

"They are for *both* of us," Debbie had answered. "But if you want *our* surprise to happen, then you must stay quiet about the boxes. You can't tell anyone about them. The boxes will be our little secret. Okay, Sus?"

"Okay, Mommy," she had agreed.

But the excitement and mystery had been more than the little girl could stand. She had told her preschool teacher about the boxes. After all, Susanna felt very close to Ms. Atkins. She could not imagine what could be wrong about telling her beloved teacher 'the secret'.

Debbie found out about her daughter's loose mouth when she came to pick Susanna up from preschool that day. While she waited for Susanna and some other children to put up their crayons and papers for the day, in colorful plastic blocks, Ms. Atkins had spilled the beans.

"So Susanna tells me there are a lot of boxes sitting around your house. Are you getting ready to move?" The teacher asked. She was asking both out of curiosity, and because of the fact that there would be an opening at the preschool if Debbie and Susanna moved away. Tiny Tykes Academy always had a waiting list. It was considered to be an excellent preschool.

Debbie stared at the young teacher's pale blue eyes. Ms. Atkins had only been out of college a year. And her freckled face – going along well with her long, flaming red hair – made her seem even younger. So did her high-pitched vocal range – perfect with the children; irritating with adults.

I could crush this little pipsqueak so easily, Debbie found herself hatefully thinking. *She should be taught about sticking her nose into other people's business.*

Debbie's silence and her icy stare had Ms. Atkins rethinking her question. "I'm sorry," she apologized. "It's none of my business whether you are moving or not. I just wondered because Susanna brought it up."

"We aren't moving," Debbie finally said. "The boxes are for a local charity – some old toys of Susanna's. I didn't want to tell her because I knew she would be upset. But she has far more toys than she needs," Debbie artfully lied.

"Oh…okay," Ms. Atkins said with laugh. But something in her eyes gave Debbie the impression that she had not bought her story.

Ms. Atkins is forever silent now. So I don't have to worry about what she believed or didn't, Debbie thought with some satisfaction, a smile appearing on her face. She had gone into the kitchen and was sitting at the table drinking some water. *When I finish my drink, I'll pack one more box, and then I'll call it a night*, she planned. *I'll be out of Hendersonville very soon*, she pondered with satisfaction.

Her life in Hendersonville and Nashville had been peaceful and murder free for a while. Debbie was convinced she could live that way someplace else again. The Nashville area packed too much heat for her now. *My life with Susanna has to come first. She is what is most important in my life.* She gave herself a silent pep talk, as Dr. Cleaver had taught her. That is, before he had lost his mind. Debbie downed the rest of her water, pushed her chair back, and stood. She headed back into the living room to pack another box – *another box toward freedom.*

Chapter 25

Gotcha

A week later, Sherri finally received the envelope containing the results of Debbie Gray's DNA testing. She opened the manila envelope very slowly, nervous about what the report might contain. If the DNA did *not* match, they would be back to square one in this investigation. But if it *did* match, she would have their killer. There was a lot riding on the results of these tests.

Sherri pulled forth the paper detailing the outcome of the forensic testing. Allowing her eyes to peruse the results, her breath caught in her throat. She was on the telephone within seconds.

* * * *

Scott walked out the front door of the office of his current employer, Hanson's Insurance. He had just dropped off videotaped evidence of another insurance fraud case and had collected a fat check from them. He was bouncing across the parking lot when his cell phone rang.

Pulling the phone from his pocket, Scott glanced at his caller ID and saw that it was Sherri. He smiled as he opened the phone, taking her call. "Hello, beautiful. What's up?" he asked, a jovial ring to his voice.

Scott had just left her house in Tennessee early that morning. They traded nights back and forth at one another's houses now. The only time they were parted was when Sherri had her daughter. She had yet to introduce Scott into Angela's life.

"I just got off the phone with the DA's office," Sherri announced, sounding excited. Scott could almost hear laughter in her voice.

"And what case might you be calling on?" he asked, stopping beside his van.

Scott squinted into the hot, summer, late-afternoon sunshine, and watched cars whiz by on the busy highway in front of him, stirring heat from the asphalt. He also waited with growing anticipation for Sherri's next words.

"You know what case, Scott," Sherri maintained. "The DNA results came today, and Debbie Gray and Jeanette Peterson are a confirmed...one-hundred percent....match!" she declared, raising her voice an octave with exhilaration. Sherri was so happy and excited she could hardly sit still.

Scott heard a male voice in the background say, "Hey...congrats, Sherri!" Then he heard shuffling about, giggling, and a slapping noise.

"Who's celebrating with you?" Scott asked, a little envious. He wanted to be the one there with Sherri to share in her joy.

"Oh...that's my partner Newton," Sherri replied. "He's wanted this perp caught pretty badly too," she shared. "He was just givin' me a high-five of congratulations. We got her, Scott! Can you believe it? The DA is workin' on gettin' me an arrest warrant as we speak."

"Sweet!" Scott exclaimed, balling his fists and shaking his hands in front of him in elation. "I'm on my way to Hendersonville. Can I go with you to serve the warrant?"

"Uh...much as I'd love to say 'yes', Scott...you need to let us handle the arrest," Sherri said. But she also added, "I will call you as soon as I get the warrant though."

"So, in other words...I can't be right there beside you. But I could be waiting around in the wings, watching," Scott suggested with a conspiring chuckle.

Sherri heard a door slam, a chiming, a radio, and an engine starting up, so she guessed Scott was in his van with the motor running. Her only reply to his proposal was, "I'll call you in a bit."

"I'll be awaiting your call," he told her. "Should you serve the warrant before I can get to Hendersonville, you be careful. Jeanette is very dangerous," Scott reminded her, sounding concerned.

"I've been a detective for over two years, Scott, and a police officer even longer than that. I know how to take care of myself," Sherri reminded him, her independent streak alive and well.

"That much I know," he agreed with an amused chuckle. "But I have a personal stake in your welfare. You happen to be the woman I love. So you'll have my worry whether you want me to or not," he told her.

"I love you too, Scott," she responded in a quiet voice, smiling. It felt good to honestly profess these words to him. And it felt equally as grand to hear him say them to her and believe that Scott meant what he was saying. "I'll see you in a bit."

"It can't be too soon for me," he answered.

Scott had already maneuvered his van out of the parking lot and onto Dixie Highway. He was zooming, posthaste, past shopping centers, auto repair shops and other commercial shops. He was headed to the Watterson Expressway and I-65 after that. He could not wait to get to Hendersonville and see Jeanette finally get what was coming to him. Jeanette would be behind bars in a short while, at long last. Scott stepped down harder on the accelerator, propelling the van toward Hendersonville, Sherri, and justice.

* * * *

When Scott arrived in Hendersonville, he still had not gotten a call back from Sherri. Knowing all too well how slow the justice system could move, he figured it was taking a while for the DA to obtain the warrant from a judge. He headed on to

Debbie Gray's house, guessing she might be there since it was now evening.

Parking his van across the street from Debbie's house, Scott took note of a grey cargo van backed into the driveway. It was sitting by the garage. He took out his cell phone and called Sherri. She answered almost immediately, sounding eager. "Sergeant Ball," she said.

Scott's heart sped up a beat. He still loved the sound of Sherri's sultry, southern voice. "Hello, Serge, this is your favorite PI," he said in jest.

"And where might my favorite PI be?" Sherri asked, sounding happy and carefree.

"I'm sitting in my van across the street from Debbie Gray...or should I say Jeanette Peterson's...house," he replied. "What's the status on Jeanette's arrest warrant?"

"Believe it or not...the DA was tied up on some big case in Gallatin. I have a serial killer runnin' free in Hendersonvill', and I have to take a backseat to Gallatin. Even though Hendersonvill' is a big part of Sumner County, we still always take a backseat to Gallatin," Sherri complained, sounding more than a little aggravated.

"So what does that mean? Is the DA going to get you an arrest warrant or not?" Scott probed.

"Yes. I just called for the ninety-ninth-hundredth time, and I've been told the arrest warrant is now on its way. It should be delivered anytime now. So you just hang tight."

"Easier said than done," Scott commented, sounding impatient.

"Just know that you won't have to wait much longer," Sherri promised. "I'll be there shortly. And Jeanette Peterson will be behind bars before you can shake a stick two times."

"Sounds good," Scott replied. "See ya' soon. Be safe; I love you."

"I love you too," she professed, a dreamy rhythm to her voice.

The two had no more than hung up when Scott spied a glimpse of Debbie Gray around the back of the house. She was carrying a box and heading toward the rear of the van. "Oh crap!" he swore, his insides knotting up. *Jeanette's on to us. He's packing boxes into the back of that van. He may be about to fly the coop again*, Scott instantly concluded, flustered.

He watched Debbie load a few more boxes into the back of the van. Then he heard her closing the doors. He watched as Debbie opened the passenger side door, walked to the back of the house to get a booster seat, and began securing this seat in the van. *She's getting ready to leave*, Scott noted with panic. He clicked off options in his mind: *I could follow Debbie and let the police know her exact location. Or I can act alone now!*

Scott had been waiting almost two years for this day. He did not want to give Jeanette any chance of escaping justice once more. His mind was quickly made up. *I need to stop this monster from leaving at any cost.*

With this plan in mind, Scott started his van. He put it in reverse and backed up a short distance. Then he put it in drive and turned into Debbie's driveway. He pulled his van up to the front of Debbie's, pinning in her vehicle. The only way Debbie would be able to move would be to go through Scott's van – a feat not so readily accomplished.

Hearing his van pull into the driveway, Debbie Gray looked out the windshield at him. She fiddled around for a few more moments inside before she vacated her van, slamming the door. She had a puzzled expression on her face as she stared at Scott's van. As she approached his van and could more fully make him out through his darkened front windshield, her expression turned to one of shock.

Debbie dared to walk up to his driver door and knock on the window. Scott debated his next course of action. *Should I roll down the window or should I just sit here and let Jeanette play his cards? The Hendersonville PD is bound to be here soon.* In the end, temptation got the better of Scott.

He pressed his finger down on the automatic window button and the motor buzzed as the glass barrier between him and Jeanette slowly disappeared. He was face to face with him now. Scott wanted to reach out and throttle this immoral criminal, but he fought this primal urge.

"Hello, Jeanette," Scott growled, staring him down. "We meet again at long last."

"I should have figured," Jeanette strangely replied, shaking her head. "So you're the one doing this to me," she commented. "Guess it's payback time for killing your girlfriend."

"For killing Debbie – who you even had the gall to call yourself. And for all the others you've killed," Scott replied with disgust. "And yes…your ass being thrown in prison once and for all will be a great payback. It will be even sweeter if you get the death penalty."

"Brutal slayings in not just one…but *two* states… you've just about assured that. Haven't you?" Jeanette questioned. Her arms were on her hips, and her evil eyes bore into Scott's.

"What do you mean *I've* assured that? You're the smarmy bastard that lives to kill. You were hidden away here in Tennessee. You might not have been caught for many more years…if then…but you just could not forgo your thirst for blood…."

"So you've made it appear," Jeanette interrupted with a smirk.

"What kind of crap are you talking?" Scott asked. The ring of his cell phone diverted his attention. It was lying on the seat beside him. Scott glanced over to try and see the number.

This lapse of attention was all Jeanette needed. Jeanette's elbow slammed into Scott's head; darkness instantly enveloped him.

Chapter 26

Empty Nest

Sherri was surprised when she got Scott's voicemail. *Wonder why he isn't answering his cell phone*, she pondered with slight concern. She thought about calling again, but thought better of it. *I've got the arrest warrant. I'm on my way, so Scott will just see me when I get there*, she concluded.

Sherri hightailed it out of her office, heading to the lobby to partner with Patrolman Shawn O'Brien and to wait for a social worker to arrive from Social Services. Shawn would be her back-up in the arrest. Sherri could hardly wait to put the handcuffs on Debbie Gray a.k.a. Jeanette Peterson. Making this collar would mark her finest hour as a detective with the Hendersonville Police Department. Sherri was proud to be getting this horrible mass murderer off the streets once and for all.

* * * *

Shortly thereafter, Sherri pulled her black LeSabre into Debbie Gray's driveway. Shawn pulled his squad car up by the curb in front of the house. He did not have his lights on. They were trying to be as inconspicuous as possible.

As Sherri climbed from her car, she surveyed the street, looking for Scott's van. She spied a man washing his car in a driveway across the way. She saw and heard children chattering and riding their bikes in the street. She caught sight of a woman on the sidewalk walking her dog. She observed another woman watering flowers two doors down. But Sherri saw no sign of Scott or his van.

She was surprised – and worried – about this turn of events. Sherri could not imagine why Scott might have left. He had been so anxious to see her arrest Debbie Gray.

"Everything okay, Sergeant?" Officer O'Brien asked, interrupting her anxious thoughts. Having vacated his squad car, he had walked up the driveway and stood beside Sherri now. Martha Ryan, an older woman from Social Services, who had ridden with Sherri to Debbie's house, was also outside with Sherri and Officer O'Brien. She was standing at Sherri's other side. Both Shawn and Martha were looking expectantly at Sherri to dictate their next move.

Sherri looked into Shawn's young, fresh face. He reminded her of a tall, skinny, blond version of Ron Howard in *Happy Days*. In his police uniform, he almost looked like a little boy playing dress up. "Everything's fine, Shawn," she answered. "There's a van in the driveway, so I'm assumin' someone is home. Let's go serve our warrant," she directed, sounding no-nonsense.

"Let's do it," he agreed, eager for some action.

Shawn followed Sherri up the front walk, and Martha Ryan fell in behind him. Shawn and Martha stopped just shy of the stairs. Keeping watch over Sherri, Shawn unsnapped his hip holster and fingered his gun. Should there be any trouble, he would draw in a second and shoot if need be.

Sherri climbed the stairs, rang the doorbell, and knocked on the door. She waited impatiently for some response. The door did not have a window, so she could not see in. A few moments later, a young, slender, blond-haired teenage girl in off-the-hip jeans and a short T-shirt came to the door. A much smaller girl peeked out from behind her. Sherri was surprised to find a teenager in the house.

"Hi," Sherri greeted. "Is Debbie Gray home?" she asked.

The teen looked past Sherri to the older, rounded, grey-haired lady in a black polyester suit, and the tall, slim, blond, uniformed policeman standing on the sidewalk. She also noted the squad car out front. "Is something wrong?" she asked with a furrowed brow.

"Hi," the smaller girl chirped, pushing herself in front of the older girl. She smiled up at Sherri, appearing fearless of this stranger at her door.

Sherri smiled down at this charming little angel – black curly hair, long lashes, large and innocent brown eyes, dressed in an adorable, frilly, pink sun suit. Sherri wanted to scoop the girl up and take her to raise with her own daughter. Instead, sadness tugged at Sherri's heartstrings as she realized this trusting little girl would soon be going to Social Services with grandmotherly Martha Ryan, to be placed with a foster family.

"Susanna, you need to go and play," the unidentified blonde said to her. She lightly clutched the little girl's shoulders, turned her little body, and gave her a shove toward some toys lying in the living room floor. "Go," she ordered in a stern voice, pointing.

Susanna reluctantly headed in that direction, even though she was more interested in the people standing on and around her front porch. "I'm Gayle, Susanna's babysitter," the teen explained, directing her attention back to Sherri. "May I ask who you are?" Gayle eyeballed Sherri now, noting she was dressed in a stylish pantsuit. She also liked this older woman's hairstyle and makeup.

"I'm Sergeant Sherri Ball," she answered, extracting her badge and holding it up so the teen could see it. "I take it bein's you're here that Ms. Gray is not," Sherri surmised, looking past the girl into the house. She saw no other sign of movement, and the rest of the house looked dark.

"Ms. Gray *was* here. I was watching Susanna while she loaded things into the van out back. Ms. Gray left with some man in another van a little while ago. She said she would be back soon," Gayle freely relayed.

"What did this other van look like, Gayle? Did you see it?" Sherri asked, her heart beginning to race.

"Yeah, I saw it. It was pulled right up beside the house and the side window. I looked out when I heard a man's voice. The van was blue," Gayle replied.

"Did...did the van have darkened windows on the side?" Sherri asked, beginning to sweat. The day was humid, but her perspiration was not from the heat.

"Yeah," Gayle confirmed, nodding her head. "The front windows were really dark too. But the man driving had his side window down, so I did see him. He was a tall, nice-looking man with black hair," she volunteered.

Sherri felt sick to her stomach. "Did you see anything else, Gayle? Were Debbie and this man fightin'?" she continued to question.

"Susanna pulled me off to her room to get some toys. Then the next thing I knew, Ms. Gray came in and asked if I would stay with Susanna for a while. She said she would pay me twenty-five dollars. Then a few seconds later, I saw the blue van pulling out of the driveway," she freely shared, pointing to the driveway and the street.

"Who was drivin'?" Sherri asked.

"I don't know. I couldn't tell. The windows were too dark," Gayle answered. Then scrunching up her face, she logically conjectured, "I guess the guy was driving, since it was his van."

"Thank you for bein' so helpful, Gayle," Sherri acknowledged, trying to keep her voice from quivering. "Martha," she called, turning to look toward the older woman.

Sherri and Martha traded places then – Sherri going down the steps and Martha ascending them. "Hello, Gayle. I'm Martha Ryan," she introduced herself to the teen. "I'm with Social Services. I have a court order to take Susanna Gray into custody."

"What?!" the girl asked, her eyes growing large. "I'm just the babysitter. I'm not even eighteen yet. Like I said, Ms. Gray isn't home," she rattled.

"I realize that," Martha said in a calm voice. "But we need to take the child with us. These officers are here with an arrest warrant for Ms. Gray. She is very dangerous. You need to go home, and tell your parents what has happened. Officer O'Brien will give you a ride to your house. If you should see Debbie Gray, then you…or your parents…need to call the police ASAP."

Tears immediately sprang to Gayle's eyes. It was obvious she was very distraught and unsure of what to do. Fidgeting with a chain hanging around her neck, she asked, "C…can I go call my parents before you take Susanna?"

"As I said…Officer O'Brien will take you *to* your parents," Martha repeated, still talking in a very tranquil, straightforward manner. She pulled forth the court order. Holding it up where the scared teen could see it, Martha pointed to it and explained, "This is a legal document that gives me the right to take the child. Can you let me pass, please?"

Trembling and beginning to sob, Gayle stepped aside and allowed Martha Ryan to enter. She watched as Martha went over to Susanna and bent down to talk with her. Susanna was playing with some blocks.

Sherri came back up on the porch. "It'll be okay, Gayle," she tried to reassure the frightened teen. She placed an arm around her shoulder and began leading her out the door and down the steps toward Officer O'Brien.

Sherri turned Gayle over to Shawn and allowed him to lead the girl away to his squad car. She, in turn, hurried away to her own car. Scrambling inside, Sherri grabbed her radio transmitter. Pushing a button on the side, she called dispatch, putting out an A.P.B. on Debbie Gray. She gave a description of Scott's van, letting it be known that the van was registered to Kentucky resident Scott Arnold. Sherri informed the station that Debbie Gray had last been seen leaving her residence in this van. Sherri also alerted the station that the van's owner, Scott Arnold, might now be a hostage of Debbie Gray.

As Sherri ended her call to the station, she lowered her head and said a quick prayer that Scott was *merely* a hostage of Debbie's.

Knowing full well what Debbie was capable of, Sherri feared far worse where Scott was concerned. *Why would Scott have been in her driveway with his window down?* Sherri could not help but wonder with frustration.

Her thoughts were interrupted as Martha Ryan opened up the rear passenger door and sat pretty little Susanna in a booster seat they had brought. As Martha snapped the buckles around Susanna's tiny body, and the girl looked about the unfamiliar car at the strange faces, her lips began to quiver.

"It's okay, sweetie," Sherri said in a soothing voice, reaching to pat the girl's small, soft arm.

As Susanna began to cry, tears threatened for Sherri as well. In a flash, she had gone from the extreme high of ridding the streets of a mass murderer to the extreme low of dealing with two frightened girls and fearing for Scott's life. Sherri just wanted to stop the world and get off.

"Sergeant Ball, are you okay?" she heard Martha ask, as she slammed the back door.

Martha had climbed into the back seat behind Sherri and sat beside Susanna, trying to calm the girl. She had taken a few of Susanna's blocks from the living room floor, and she was shaking these back in forth in front of the child to try and distract her, and dissipate her fear.

Sherri took a deep breath, trying to squelch her fears. *Scott has to be okay*, she tried to convince herself. *Me having a meltdown isn't going to help him. I need to pull myself together and find Debbie Gray ASAP!*

"I'm fine," Sherri told Martha with more confidence than she felt.

Sherri turned her body to the front and reached to pull and snap her seatbelt in place. Starting the car, she continued her pep talk, *I'll find Scott, and he'll be okay.*

Her hopes newly confirmed, Sherri threw the car into reverse and headed out. There was no time to be wasted.

Chapter 27

The Leak

That evening, Newton came into his and Sherri's office area and stood beside her with a lost-puppy-dog look on his face.

"What's wrong?" she asked, looking up at him, instantly alarmed. Sherri thought maybe Newton had learned something about Scott.

Reaching to toy with his short tie, Newton divulged, "I was just in the lounge, and guess what was on the TV?"

"I don't want to guess, Newton. Just tell me, now!" Sherri demanded through gritted teeth, shaking her finger at him as if he were a naughty child. Seeing him back up a step, she added in a less distraught voice, with pleading eyes, "Please."

"You're not gonna like it, Sherri," he said, pushing his glasses back on his face.

"Did you hear somethin' about Scott?" Sherri asked, cutting to the chase.

"Not exactly," Newton replied, blinking his eyes. He had a nervous twitch and he was still hesitant to reveal everything.

"Newton, either tell me, or shut up!" Sherri barked, her eyes blazing. Getting information out of this man was like pulling teeth, and Sherri was frightened and irritable, in no mood for this hindrance.

"It's all over the news that the police are on the lookout for serial killer Debbie Gray, and that she has a hostage with her. They gave a description of her and Scott and even showed a picture of Scott's van. They also reported that her little girl had been taken into protective custody." Newton finally spilled the beans, looking sheepish as he squeezed his hands together at his waist.

"Oh no!" Sherri exclaimed, bringing her hands up to her face and dropping her head into them for a few moments. Sliding her hands down from her face, she folded her hands at her chin, looked up at Newton, and rhetorically asked, "How could this have happened?"

"We obviously have a leak somewhere," Newton replied. He walked around to his desk and took a seat. "I'm sorry, Sherri," he said with sympathetic eyes, addeding, "But maybe we should look on the bright side. Maybe we'll get lucky and Debbie Gray won't hear the news, and she'll go back home for her little girl after all."

Sherri did not hear Newton's last statement. Her mind was still stuck on his first – *'We obviously have a leak somewhere'*. She spun around and picked up her phone, punching numbers in with a vengeance. A second later, Geoffrey answered his phone.

"Homicide. Lieutenant Gregory speaking," he said.

"Hello, Lieutenant," Sherri said in a stern voice. "This is Sergeant Ball."

"Sherri, you don't have to be so formal. I know the last time we spoke things were a bit tense between us. But we both have officers out on the street looking for the same killer now. You did a great job gathering evidence linking this woman – or should I say man – to your Hendersonville murder and our Nashville ones. I'm proud of you for sticking to your guns," he bragged.

"Are you now?" she challenged. "And what about Scott? You'd still like to see him hung out to dry, wouldn't you, Geoff?"

"Seems like Mr. Arnold did a good enough job of doing that himself," Geoff zinged back, sounding very uncaring and unconcerned. "That's why *only* detectives should be involved in homicide cases."

"And what about this leak to the media – media incidentally comin' out of Nashville?" Sherri questioned. "Someone provided them with information about Debbie Gray. They are broadcastin' that she is bein' sought by police and that her daughter's been taken into police custody. I'm wonderin' if you had anything to do with that."

"As we said when we last parted, Sherri…you run your case the way you see fit and I'll run mine," Geoffrey commented, sounding smug.

"You son-of-a-bitch!" Sherri screamed, slamming her fists down on her desk. Her whole desk shook.

Newton's head popped up and he stared at Sherri. *Guess she located the leak*, he figured. He was alertly listening to her conversation now.

"We have an unmarked car waitin' at Debbie Gray's house for her to return for her little girl," Sherri revealed. She continued, hardly taking a breath, "But now, since it's been broadcast that her daughter is with Protective Services, she has no reason to return home. You've further endangered Scott's life and the lives of all the citizens you serve. I hope you are really proud of yourself, Geoff!"

"First off, Scott endangered his own life. He should *not* have been anywhere near Debbie Gray. He should have left that to the professionals – you and I. And as to releasing information about Debbie Gray to the media, I did that to *protect* the citizens I serve. *Now*, there is a good chance one of them will see her – or Scott's van – and call MNPD. Then we'll have Debbie Gray behind bars. Keeping the information hidden only *puts* citizens in the line of danger. You should have kept Scott Arnold out of the realm of danger, Sherri. If anyone is to blame for him being in harm's way, it is you," Lt. Gregory very pointedly stated.

His words were like a knife to Sherri's heart. She could not debate them. She *did* blame herself for Scott's current predicament. *He* shouldn't *have been anywhere close to her*, she concluded, in agony. Tears suddenly threatened.

"Fuck you, Geoff!" she replied, slamming down her phone receiver.

Sherri leapt to her feet and dashed toward the women's restroom. She did not want to break down in front of Newton. She had never been so frightened or remorseful in her life.

Chapter 28

The Call

Sherri spent a sleepless night worrying about Scott. The early-morning news aired another plea for citizens to be on the lookout for Debbie Gray and Scott's blue van with Kentucky plates. They even gave the plate number.

Sherri arrived at work looking worse for wear. Her hair was not styled, hanging limp and lifeless. Wearing little to no makeup, her face was pale and dark circles shone under her eyes. Even her impeccable fashion sense was compromised. Her clothes were wrinkled, almost as if Sherri had slept in them. Her personal appearance was the last thing on her mind. Sherri's sole objective was to find Debbie Gray and save Scott's life. She knew the more hours that passed the fewer chance of Scott's safe return.

Sherri had been at her desk about an hour when her phone rang. She snatched it up, hoping for the hundredth time that it might be someone calling with news of Debbie Gray and/or Scott.

"Sergeant Ball," she spit out. She hung on the edge of her seat, waiting for someone to answer back. The second it took seemed to last hours.

"Sherri, it's Nelson Reardon."

Nelson? Gaylord precinct. Why is he calling? Sherri took a half second to ponder. Taking a deep breath, she curtly asked, "What is it, Nelson?" She feared what he would say next.

"She...um, Debbie Gray...has struck again," he revealed.

Sherri's heart began to race and her stomach churned. Her hand trembled as she squeezed the phone. *Is Nelson calling me because Debbie has killed Scott?* Sherri wondered. She could not muster the courage to ask.

"Sherri, are you still there?" Nelson asked.

"Y…yeah," she managed to stutter, tears springing to her eyes.

"Geoff asked me to call you as a professional courtesy," he continued.

There was a roar in Sherri's head and tears began to course down her cheeks.

Newton noticed Sherri was crying. "Sherri," he said. "What's up?"

She held the receiver out to him. She could not bear to hear another word. As Newton took the phone, stretching it over to his desk, Sherri dropped her head into her lap and, brokenhearted, began to sob.

She did not hear much of what Newton had to say because she was so distraught. A few moments later, she felt Newton's hand rubbing her back. His caring touch caused Sherri to cry even more. *He's showing his sympathy*, she concluded. She felt bad, because she spent a lot of time aggravated with this man. Newton was a good detective, but he was very slow and precise with everything he did.

"Sherri," she heard him calling in a soft, consoling voice.

She slowly raised her head. Newton gradually came into view despite her tear-stained eyes. He was looking down at her with concern.

"Don't say it, Newton. I…I already know," Sherri stated, holding her palm up. Her lips trembled and more tears escaped.

"Sherri, it's not what you think," he told her, squeezing her shoulder.

"What do you mean?" she asked, her brow furrowing. She allowed herself a small glimmer of hope.

"It *wasn't* Scott," Newton was happy to divulge. His lips even curved a bit.

"It...Newton, are you sure?" Sherri asked, disbelieving.

"Sherri, I'm positive," he maintained, giving her shoulder a reassuring pat. "It was a secretary for a psychiatrist in Nashville. It was a *woman*, Sherri. Not even close to bein' Scott," he said with a happy snicker. Then he added with a somber expression, "Not that I'm happy Debbie Gray killed again."

"But...Newton.... Nelson Reardon...he...he said he was callin' me as a professional courtesy," Sherri revealed, still having a hard time believing Newton's words. She wanted them to be true more than life itself, but she did not want to get her hopes up only to have them squelched again.

"It *is* a professional courtesy for those guys to share anything with us," Newton pointed out with an aggravated smirk.

"Those assholes!" Sherri cursed, beating a fist in her lap.

"Yeah...exactly," Newton agreed with a grin. "Sherri, why don't you go to the lounge for awhile? I'll sit at your desk and take your calls."

"Thanks, Newton," she said, forcing a grateful smile. "But I'll be fine. I've got hope again. And I've also got work to do. I need to call Nelson back and get more details on this latest homicide. Why would Debbie Gray kill again, knowin' police are on her trail? I could see her killin' Scott...to make a statement. But this new murder makes no sense," she commented, becoming more and more rational and thinking like a detective again.

"Who knows what logic serial killers use," Newton commented, shrugging his shoulders.

He was glad to see that Sherri had regained her composure. But his worry had not dissipated. Newton realized there was still a good possibility that Scott Arnold would turn up dead. He could see no reason why Debbie Gray would choose to show Scott any mercy. Newton guessed that Sherri had already concluded the same thing, especially considering how she had overreacted to Nelson Reardon's call.

"How about I go get you some coffee then," Newton offered.

"Coffee sounds great," Sherri replied, giving him another smile. "Thanks, Newton. For everything."

"Hey…what are partners for?" he downplayed. He headed away to get Sherri a cup of hot coffee to warm her insides and settle her nerves.

Chapter 29

The Van

That evening, Sherri picked up her daughter for the weekend. Even though Sherri was glad to spend time with her precious little girl, her mind was too preoccupied about Scott to fully enjoy Angela's presence.

After Sherri put Angela to bed for the night – about 10:00 p.m. – she retired to her own room to try and get some rest. She crawled under a blanket and hugged a pillow, wishing this inanimate object was Scott. Tossing and tumbling, Sherri finally fell into a fitful sleep. She awoke with a start about 5:00 a.m. Saturday morning. Her gut told her to call the station.

Newton answered his phone on the second ring. "Homicide, this is Newton," he said, sounding distracted. Newton was a worker bee; he was always busy fiddling with something at his desk.

"Newton, it's Sherri," she told him. She was still lying in bed in the dark with her bedside phone cradled at her ear.

"Sherri, this is supposed to be your weekend off. You're supposed to be spending a few days with your daughter. What in blazes are you doin' up so early and callin' in here?" he scolded. Newton wanted Sherri to get some R and R. He was concerned about her having a breakdown if she did not start to take better care of herself.

"Newton, you know why I'm callin'," Sherri replied. "What's the latest on Debbie Gray and Scott?" she asked, getting right to the point.

"How do you know there is a 'latest'?" he asked, being deliberately evasive.

Sherri slid to a sitting position in the bed. "Newton, what aren't you tellin' me?" she inquired, clutching her blanket up to her chin as if she were cold.

"Sherri...they...a...they found Scott's van," he reluctantly let slide off his tongue.

Sherri released her blanket and kicked it from her body. She slid her legs sideways and was now sitting on the side of the bed. Her hand was like a vice on the phone, and she demanded, "And? Come on, Newton, dammit! Give me some details. Why didn't you call me?"

"There's not a lot to share, Sherri," he downplayed.

"Newton, I didn't call you at freakin' five a.m. in the mornin' to be given the run-around," Sherri growled in a low voice. She did not want to get too loud and wake up Angela; although, thankfully, her daughter was a deep sleeper.

With nervous, aggravated energy, Sherri stood and took long strides over to the window across the room. Pulling back a sheer curtain, she stared aimlessly out at her dark front yard, watching the breeze stir some tree limbs and listening to the birds' early-morning piercing chirps. "Please tell me everything, Newton," she said in a pleading voice.

"The only thing that matters is that Scott is still assumed to be alive, Sherri," he finally replied, adding, "We've found no sign to indicate otherwise. His van was ditched in the parking lot of the Charlotte Pike Wal-Mart. The store was searched, but there was no sign of Debbie or Scott. The dumpsters in the back of the store were also searched, and nothing of significance was found. There was a little blood in the van...."

"Whoa!" Sherri screeched, jerking back from the window. Releasing the curtain, it settled back closed. "Back up one second! You found blood in the van," she repeated, standing frozen, white-knuckling the phone. "How is that *insignificant*?"

"Because there was not that much blood, Sherri," Newton tried to console her.

"I take it the blood was fresh," she further clarified. A hot summer's night, the air conditioner kicked on and was blowing cold air directly across her bare feet and legs. Sherri shivered; although it was not the cool air that was making her cold.

"It was fairly fresh...yeah," Newton clarified. "It's been sent for DNA testin' so we'll know soon whether it belongs to either Debbie or Scott. The thing is...Scott could have cut himself shavin' and there would have been this much blood, Sherri. His van was not a murder site," he tried to reassure her.

"Well...to the best of my knowledge, Scott doesn't shave in his van," Sherri contradicted, sounding sassy. When Newton did not immediately reply, Sherri reigned in her anger and apologized, "Sorry. I don't mean to be cross with you, Newton...."

"Sherri, you don't need to apologize to me," he was quick to assure her. "I know you are goin' out of your mind with worry over Scott. And believe me...if I really had anything to tell you, I would have called. But we pretty much are still at square one. And that's not a really awful place to be right now."

He means it's better than Scott being dead, Sherri concluded.

"Sherri, why don't you climb in bed and try to get some sleep," Newton helpfully suggested. "Have you gotten any sleep at all?"

"Yeah...I slept for a few hours," she told him. "But I can't see me goin' back to sleep any time soon," she shared. She walked over and plopped down on the side of the bed, reaching to grab her blanket and wrap it around her legs.

"See why I didn't call you," Newton defended his position. "There is nothin' you can do, Sherri. There is nothin' any of us can do right now...it's watch and wait from here. Now, please, try and get some rest. You won't be any good to Scott at all if you let yourself get run down and sick."

"Nice argument," she agreed with a sigh of surrender, reaching to rub her forehead. "Get back to work, Newt. You be sure and call me if anything new develops."

"If anything really *significant* develops, I *will* call you," he pledged.

"Alright," Sherri hesitantly agreed. "I'll see ya' Monday."

"See ya," Newton replied. "Have a good weekend with you daughter."

"I'll try," Sherri promised. "Bye."

"Bye," Newton responded, ending the call.

As Sherri placed her phone back on the charger, she laid back down in bed, more worried and frustrated than ever. She wanted to go out and scour the streets until she apprehended Debbie Gray and brought Scott home safe. But she knew her thinking was foolish. Everyone was doing everything they could. Newton was right. The most they could do now was watch and wait. Sherri was frustrated beyond reason by her helplessness.

Chapter 30

Final Session

Dr. Cleaver had a temporary new office. He had been moved to a small conference room within the same building by the landlord. The receptionist area of his usual office space was being revamped after Marissa's brutal slaying. The old, bloodstained carpet was being removed and new carpet was being laid. Also, Marissa's chair and desk were being replaced. These items were both saturated with blood as well.

It was Monday – midmorning – and Dr. Cleaver was awaiting a new patient – a woman by the name of Renee O'Riley. His secretary from a temp agency – an African-American woman named Rochelle Davis – beeped him on his intercom. She was sitting at a card table in the hall just outside the door to the conference room. On the table, she had a computer monitor, keyboard, mouse, and a phone with an intercom. Her hard drive was under the table at her feet.

"Yes, Rochelle," Dr. Cleaver answered.

"Renee O'Riley is here to see you, doctor," she replied.

"Send her in," Dr. Cleaver directed.

"Okay," Rochelle replied.

Forgetting to take her finger off the intercom button, Dr. Cleaver could hear her say, "You can go right in, Ms. O'Riley." Then a second later, he heard a beep and figured the woman had finally released the intercom button. Good help was hard to find, and Wally knew Marissa would be missed. He had hated that she had to die.

A moment later, Dr. Cleaver's door opened. A chubby woman with short, spiked, bleach-blond hair entered, shut the door behind her and leaned against it. Wally noticed her dark complexion. She looked as if she had been to a tanning bed or had just gotten back from Florida. Through her glasses, something seemed familiar about her bright-blue eyes, but Wally was not sure what.

"Hello, Ms. O'Riley," Wally greeted, folding his hands over his belly. "What can I do for you today?"

He was seated behind a small conference room table in a short-backed, cloth, office chair with padded arms. He had a phone with an intercom, a box of tissues, a pitcher of water – with no ice – and some glasses sitting on the table. Directly in front of him, he had a notepad and a pen.

Ms. O'Riley smiled, and something else sparked a trace of familiarity with Dr. Cleaver. *Who does this woman remind me of?* He found himself pondering, folding his hands and putting his index fingers up to his lips.

When she spoke, it all became clear in a flash. "Hello, Wally," she said. Dr. Cleaver recognized her voice. It was the voice of Debbie Gray.

"What a disguise, Debbie!" he commented, an amused smile coming to his face. "I almost didn't recognize you. But then that's the point, isn't it? What did you do to your skin? Put on some of that fake tan stuff?"

"It's amazing what you can find at Wal-Mart," she commented. She walked over to the table, rolled out a chair, and took a seat across from him. "We need to talk, Wally," she told him, staring directly into his eyes and lacing her fingers in front of her.

"Well...Ms. O'Riley paid in cash for twenty minutes, so I guess you have earned the time. No wonder she didn't have any insurance," he commented, an admiring smirk on his face. "O'Riley! Now that I think of it...wasn't that your maiden name, Jeanette?" he asked. Then, before she could respond, he added, "And Renee was the name of your first victim. You like to recycle names, don't you?"

"You've certainly done your research, Wally. How long have you known who I was? Since our first session?" she questioned.

"I started to put two and two together shortly thereafter, yeah," he answered with a proud grin, sitting back in his chair and lacing his fingers over his abdomen. "News from Louisville does travel to Bowling Green, Jeanette. I lived there for many years. When you went on the lam from Louisville, the news did a segment on your brutal murders. I was mesmerized by the story. When, during a session, Debbie graphically described how she would/wanted to kill someone, I remembered that news segment from Bowling Green."

"So? I could have just wanted to copycat that killer," Jeanette argued, her eyes still puzzled.

"Good point," Wally agreed with a grin. He joined his index fingers and pointed and shook them at Jeanette. "That's actually what I figured, and this lead to a sinister plan on my part. Why not make Debbie Gray a copycat killer? That's when I began to do more research on Jeanette *O'Riley* Peterson and her Louisville murders. In gathering my facts, I stumbled upon information that Jeanette and retired deputy sheriff Jackson Jordan were bitter enemies. I did a little research on good ol' Jack then and found out – lo and behold – he now lived in Hendersonville. Debbie Gray lived in Hendersonville...seemed like a match made in heaven to me for a first killing," he pointed out, unlacing his hands and shaking them palm down with excitement.

"So you were setting up Debbie...not Jeanette. I still don't see how you figured out I was Jeanette," she commented, her face pinched as she scratched her chin.

"I might never have known for sure until you showed up for your session after Jack's murder. You admitted to knowing the man. Then in the next session, you went into even more detail about your relationship, saying that you screwed around with good ol' Jack in, no less...*Kentucky*. As far as I was concerned, all the cards were on the table at that point. I was convinced you were Jeanette Peterson," he said with a triumphant laugh. He sat back in his chair, tapping his thumbs together at his waist and looking smug.

"I'd ask you why you didn't turn me into the cops, but I already know that answer," Jeanette told him, nodding her head in confirmation.

"And what might that answer be?" Wally baited, smiling and shaking his steepled index fingers at her again.

"Because allowing me to go free allowed you to become Jeanette Peterson, and to continue to copycat off my murders. You even wore uniform shoes when you committed the murders, so it would look like they were my shoes. You are fortunate to have small feet for a man, Wally. Wrong tread though…sorry. Oh…by the way…you should know…I never killed a victim from behind. Part of the fun is seeing the fear in their eyes when you kill them."

"Well…you can't have everything," Wally laughed and shrugged. "How'd you finally figure out I was the one copycatting off of you, Jeanette?" he asked, crossing his arms.

"All the victims were linked to me in some way. When Scott Arnold pulled in my driveway the other day, I thought it was him who had set me up," Jeanette revealed.

"Oh…speaking of Mr. Arnold, where is he? Have you killed him?" Wally asked, sounding almost jovial. He appeared to want to hear the gory details.

"Wouldn't you like to know," Jeanette sassed. "Let's just say I have special plans for Scott…dead or alive," she shared, tapping her thumbs. "Now, back to you," he said, pointing his index finger at Wally. "Marissa's death made it all clear to me who my copycat killer must be. That…and you being so crazy our last session. I had taken Scott, so I knew he could not have killed Marissa. It didn't make sense that it was him anyway. Scott Arnold is too straight eagle…but I thought… maybe the grief of losing his girlfriend had caused him to lose it. Revenge will cause a person to do strange things."

"That it will," Dr. Cleaver agreed, rubbing his knuckles together.

"So why'd you do this, Wally?" Jeanette asked, her eyes boring into Dr. Cleaver's.

With a half-smile on his face, he disclosed, "You and I are a great deal alike, Jeanette. I have enormous rage toward my parents too…or, in particular, my father. He was an abusive SOB. Wally could not handle it. He was always weak, so to keep him from breaking, I had to take over…."

"What do you mean *Wally* was weak and *you* took over?" Jeanette interrupted him, puzzled.

"Exactly what I said," Wally confirmed, leaning forward and smiling.

Jeanette pondered his words for only a second before her eyes lit up and she exclaimed, "Good Lord! Are you saying…do multiple personalities actually exist?" She questioned out loud. She had read books about this disorder, but now she had to wonder, *Is Dr. Cleaver just playing with me? He's a psychiatrist. He could use this craziness as a defense.*

"They call it Dissociative Identity Disorder nowadays," he explained, laughing. "Wally took us to a neurologist, and this doctor figured out we had this illness. I've been in control ever since. Wally is so weak he would probably have had us locked up in a mental institution. His career would go down the tubes. But I don't know how long I can continue to step into his shoes as a psychiatrist. Listening to people snivel about their pasts – like you were the other day – makes me want to puke. I think your first plan of action…killing people…was far better than sitting around 'role-playing' in some head-shrinker's office."

Jeanette stared at Dr. Cleaver – or whoever this person was sitting across from him. She thought about the diverse ways the doctor had behaved during different therapy sessions. She recalled how the doctor seemed to have lapses of memory. From reading about this bizarre disorder, Jeanette knew memory lapses were a big part of it. So were headaches, and Wally had told her he had these too.

"Unbelievable!" Jeanette exclaimed, slapping a leg. "So what is your name, and how long have you been killing?" she questioned with noted interest.

"I don't have a separate name. Although I've always thought of myself as *The Incredible Hulk*. So you can call me Hulk if you like. I come out of Wally's anger, fear, and frustration. In times of need, I take care of him. When dear ol' dad used to do unmentionables, I would come out. I'm tough as steel and can't be hurt. Wally would come back after the abuse, so he didn't feel the pain or remember the attack. He remembered enough though that he wanted to become a psychiatrist and help others find…" Hulk held his fingers up in the air, making quote signs, and continued, "'peaceable solutions' to their problems. Like I said, he's basically a weak link. But people like you buy into his crap, and he's made a good living for us. To answer your other question, the first people I killed were some folks in Bowling Green – a crazy broad, her husband and daughters. I made it look as if she had committed suicide and took out her whole family with her. That was a few years ago."

"Why'd you do it?" Jeanette asked, still curious. She was rubbing his chin.

"The broad claimed she was going to the psychiatric board on Wally. She claimed he had sexually abused her during a session. I think she was completely nuts. As far as I know, there is not a sexual predator within Wally. Unless there is another personality I don't know about. Whatever…I needed to protect Wally. He couldn't remember what happened on the day she said the rape took place, so he was ready to turn us in. I took care of the problem in another manner. Murder is a real rush, isn't it?" he stated, laughing.

Jeanette liked this other man's deviousness. It made her respect 'the Hulk'. "So where do we go from here… *Hulk*?"

she asked, resting her elbow on the padded chair arm and propping her chin up with a fist.

"Well…either one of us kills the other…or we help one another. Those seem to be our only options," Hulk replied, leaning back in his chair and tapping his fingertips together. "So what will it be, Jeanette? Do we fight to the death...or team up? I'm game for either one," he said with a wicked smile.

"I have a gun in my purse, so I could kill you fairly easily," Jeanette confessed, pulling her bag into her lap.

Hulk showed no fear. Jeanette believed he would go down with a fight, even if she pulled a gun. *At last, a worthy adversary!* she thought with a rush. "As I said, I like to see the fear in my victim's eyes. You have no fear, so what good would killing you do me?" Jeanette asked, squeezing the top of her purse.

"So how can I help you then?" Hulk asked, folding his hands and laying them over his stomach. He looked very relaxed.

"First," Jeanette said, holding his index finger up. "I need to get my daughter back. You could go to Social Services and find out where she is."

"Very easily," he said, and added with a calculating grin, "After all, I'm Debbie Gray's psychiatrist. I think I can get in to see Susanna in a heartbeat. Could we do this today? It sounds like a lot more fun then seeing patients," he said, rubbing his hands together in anticipation.

"The sooner the better," Jeanette agreed. "I'll drive you over there."

"What, don't you trust me to drive over there myself?" he asked with a chuckle.

"Let's just say I want to keep my eye on you," Jeanette replied.

"A wise idea, Jeanette. A very wise idea," he complimented, smiling in amusement and shaking his finger at him. "Well...what are we waiting for? Let's do it!" he suggested.

"Fine by me," Jeanette agreed.

She stood and watched Hulk also stand. Working with this man showed that Jeanette would work with the devil himself to get Susanna back. Jeanette did not care what happened to Hulk once he helped her escape with her daughter. Jeanette would even take the blame for the Nashville and Hendersonville murders.

She only wanted to get his daughter back, tie up some loose ends with Scott Arnold and his meddling girlfriend, Sergeant Ball, and bail from the Nashville area – never to return. She still had plenty of other identities she could take on and plenty of other states she could hide in.

The two headed out of the conference room, intent on setting their plan into action and moving on with both their lives as soon as possible.

Chapter 31

The Bridge

Late Monday afternoon, Sherri was sitting on the carpet, in the middle of the floor, in her family room, playing the board game Candy Land with Angela. She was also trying to keep her mind off of Scott. Sherri had called Newton that morning and there was still no news on Debbie or Scott. Right now, though, no news was good news as far as Scott was concerned.

Sherri's ex-husband would be picking Angela up in a few hours, and Sherri would be going into the station to work the late shift. So she was taking advantage of her last few hours with her little girl by giving her one-on-one time.

A ringing phone interrupted their tranquil playtime. "Mommy will be right back, Ang," Sherri promised with a re-assuring smile.

As if her life depended on it, she leapt to her feet and charged toward the phone on a table a few feet away. Snatching it up and turning it on, she barked in an anxious voice, "Hello!"

"Sherri, it's Newton," he said and rushed on. "Before you get all worked up...I still know nothing about Scott. As far as we all know, Scott is still fine," he assured her.

"But you do have somethin' important to tell me, or you wouldn't be callin', right?" Sherri baited, eager to hear the latest news.

"Right," Newton agreed. He paused and Sherri heard him exhale.

"What now?" she asked, guessing his news was not good.

"Susanna's been kidnapped from Social Services," he disclosed.

"What?! How?!" Sherri shouted, demanding to know. She looked over and saw Angela's wide, brown eyes staring up at her, and she realized her tone might have scared her. "Hold on a sec, Newt," Sherri said, laying the phone down on the table.

Walking back over to her daughter and bending down, Sherri said in a consoling voice, "Ang, mommy didn't mean to scream and scare you. Why don't you roll the dice and move for mommy and yourself? I'll be back in just a second. This is a very important call."

"Is it bad news, mommy?" the perceptive four year old asked. Her mommy's tired, troubled eyes worried her. Her mommy had looked sad all weekend.

Sherri reached to feather her fingers through her daughter's straight, soft, brown bangs. "It's police stuff, Ang," she answered. "Nothin' for you to be worried about. You just play, and mommy will be right back.

Sherri brought her lips to her daughter's tiny forehead and planted a soothing kiss. Angela cupped her hands around her mommy's face and gave her a kiss on the lips. "It'll be okay, mommy," she assured her.

Sherri's heart was warmed and she smiled. Her smile made all right with the world again for Angela. She had made her mommy happy, and that was all that mattered to her right now. She picked up the dice and tossed them on the board with a clunk, playing the game as her mommy had asked.

Sherri stood, picked the phone back up, walked out of the room, and shut the door behind her. "Sorry, Newton," she apologized, walking farther down the hall. "Can you give me the details of Susanna's abduction?" She picked up her conversation right where she had left off.

"I'm sorry to interrupt your private time with your daughter," he apologized. He had heard Sherri talking to Angela.

"Newton, it can't be avoided right now," Sherri assured him. "Now please stay on task! What happened?"

"It appears Debbie Gray has her psychiatrist working with her," Newton revealed.

"Her psychiatrist?!" Sherri repeated, sounding disbelieving.

"A bald, slightly overweight male, about five-foot-seven, walked into Social Services in Nashville a few hours ago. He showed credentials proving he was a licensed psychiatrist. He said that he had been treating both Debbie Gray and her daughter Susanna. He claimed he wanted to check on the child's mental state. Martha Ryan took him to see Susanna. About an hour later, Martha was found unconscious, and Susanna had disappeared. So now, MNPD has an APB out on Dr. Wallace Cleaver as well. According to Nelson Reardon, MNPD got the shrink's temp secretary to confirm that Debbie Gray *was* indeed one of his patients. I don't know why this doctor is workin' with Debbie, but he is."

"So Debbie likely has Susanna back right now," Sherri surmised. "Dammit! We just can't catch a break with this case." She wallowed, perturbed.

"I don't know, Sherri. Maybe MNPD will track down the doctor and he will be able to help lead them to Debbie. The doctor obviously doesn't have any idea what a monster she is, or he wouldn't be helpin' her."

"You're a lot more optimistic than I am right now, Newton," she admitted, sounding defeated.

"Well, all we can do right now is hope, Sherri," Newton replied.

And as long as Scott is not found dead, then I do still have hope, Sherri pondered. "Thanks for keepin' me informed, Newt. I'll be in soon," she told him.

"See ya', Sher," he said.

They ended their call then. Sherri powered off the phone, turned, and headed back to the family room. Before she opened the door, she plastered on a fake smile. She did not want her daughter to be worried or upset. She wanted the last few hours of this visit to be good ones. When she got to the station, she could let worry and frustration plague her again. But for now, Sherri was going to let Angela's beautiful face and personality cheer her.

* * * *

Sherri's first few hours at the station were pretty mundane. She was working the night shift all alone. This shift was usually pretty quiet. But at 11:50 p.m., that all changed in the blink of an eye.

Sherri's phone rang, and she answered it at once. "Sergeant Ball," she said.

"Hello, Sherri," a woman's voice replied.

Since the caller addressed her by her first name, Sherri figured it was someone who knew her, although she did not recognize the voice.

"Who's callin'?" she asked.

"Let's just say that I'm the person you took someone very dear from," the woman replied; then she added with a haunting laugh, "And I'm about to even the score. If you'd like to see your boyfriend, Scott Arnold...alive...one last time... head to the railroad bridge in Nashville. Hurry though! They run a lot of trains on that bridge," she goaded with more laughter. Then she hung up the phone.

"Oh my God!" Sherri exclaimed, the phone receiver shaking in her hand. She reached to hang it up and sprung to her feet. She knew the call had not lasted long enough to trace it. *It was Jeanette!* she recognized in horror.

There was no time to waste. Sherri needed to get to the railroad bridge, and she needed to get there *now*. She remembered what Scott had told her about Jeanette's first victim, 'Jeanette handcuffed his first victim in Kentucky to a train track and watched her get mowed down'. Sherri could not allow a sadistic rerun of this past murder to play out with Scott. Like a madwoman, she dashed from the office, forgetting all common sense and police protocol.

* * * *

Hulk loomed over Scott, having beaten him into unconsciousness. Scott lay on his back on a section of track running across the Nashville Railroad Bridge. Hulk had handcuffed him to anchors driven deep within each side of the railroad tie. Scott's wrists were also handcuffed together. They had been handcuffed since Jeanette took him captive.

The clouds cleared for a moment, and the moonlight brightly lit the bridge and the rushing river below. Looking down into Scott's face, even though Scott couldn't hear him, Hulk said aloud, "You should have stayed in Kentucky where you belonged, homeboy. You ruined my little fun with Debbie Gray. Now, it's time for me and Debbie to have some fun with you and your little love muffin. So long, Scott."

To add insult to injury, Hulk cleared his throat and spit in Scott's face. Laughing, he left him there with the spittle running off his cheek and jogged away from the bridge. He slithered down an embankment, and he waited.

* * * *

Sherri's drive into Nashville, though in actuality only about fifteen minutes, had seemed to take hours. Her LeSabre, siren blaring, skidded to a stop in the parking lot beside the Railroad Bridge. Sherri had not called the MNPD for backup. She no longer trusted Geoffrey, and she could take no chances where Scott's life was concerned. She was on her own, and Sherri was determined to succeed in saving Scott's life...or die trying.

As Sherri turned off the siren and vacated her car, the clouds parted again and moonlight shone through. She was able to make out a human silhouette stooped on the track in the middle of the bridge. She fought to scramble over a short rock ledge leading up onto the railroad track. Her low-heeled pumps were not made for climbing, so Sherri slipped and tangled with the rocks more than once. By the time she clambered to the top, her hands were scraped and bleeding, her dress pants had holes in them, and her knees were skinned. Sherri did not care about her torn skin or clothes. She only cared about getting onto the bridge and saving the man she loved.

She began running along the track toward the figure on the bridge. A strong wind coming off of the river twisted and tangled her hair. As Sherri drew closer to the person on the bridge, she could see that it was indeed Scott.

As Scott looked up at her, she could see that one entire side of his face was black and blue, one eye was swollen shut, and there was a bleeding gash by his temple. He had his hands, connected at the wrists with handcuffs, wrapped around a stake. He was desperately pulling to free himself. Sherri saw that Scott's other foot was also staked to the track.

"Sherri, what are you doing here?" he asked, panting. "Did they hurt you?" he questioned, noticing her torn pants and scraped knees.

"Did who hurt me?" she asked, noting he had used a plural when describing the attacker.

"Jeanette and her goon. She has a helper. He's the one who beat the hell out of me," he shared, pointing to his face. "He also pinned me here," Scott added, pulling again on the stake.

"Was this an overweight, medium-height, bald man?" Sherri asked.

"Yeah," Scott verified. "I'd like to be able to identify him from some mug shots, but I need to get off this bridge first," he pointed out with some urgency.

"That sounds like a plan," Sherri agreed. She recognized that the man that had assaulted Scott must be Debbie Gray's psychiatrist. His involvement with Debbie Gray kept getting more bizarre.

Sherri took off her suit jacket, stooped down, threw it over the stake on the opposite side, and began to pull and jerk back and forth with all her might. Scott pulled on the other side at the same time. Neither stake seemed to be budging.

"Sherri, has the Nashville PD been called?" Scott asked.

"No. Not yet," she was ashamed to admit.

"Well, I think you should go call them. Them and anybody else who can get these damn anchors loose," Scott advised.

He was weak from the beating he had taken and still dizzy from this most recent head injury. He did not see any way possible that he and Sherri alone were going to be able to disengage the anchors.

"I'm on it," Sherri agreed. "I'll be back in a second. I love you, Scott."

"I love you too," he said. Then he pointed out the obvious. "I'll be right here waiting. I'm not going anywhere." Scott sat down on the track, feeling overwhelmed.

Sherri turned and began racing back up the track. She jumped onto the rock ledge leading down to the parking lot. Her feet slipped out from under her, and she grimaced in pain as her tailbone slammed against a pointed stone. But Sherri did not let her pain stop her. She hit the ground running and hurried over to her car. She opened the door and jumped inside, grabbing for the radio to call for back-up support.

After Sherri got off the radio, she leaped back out of the car and headed once again toward the track. As she scrambled back up the ledge, she stopped in fright as she saw a light farther up the track. *Oh God!* She thought. *It's a train.* It would literally be minutes before the train reached the bridge.

She ran toward Scott. "Help is on the way," she said, gasping for breath. She dropped down to a stooped position and began to pull erratically at a stake.

"Sherri, what are you doing?" Scott asked. He could see panic in her eyes.

"Just help me, Scott," she begged, pulling and jerking even harder.

As he noticed Sherri's eyes looking beyond him, it suddenly dawned on Scott what might be scaring her. He turned his head and looked behind him. When he did, he saw the light of an oncoming train. *Oh, I am so screwed*, he thought with despair.

"Sherri, I want you off this bridge," Scott dictated.

"I'm not goin' anywhere without you," she argued, sweating as she jerked and pulled all the more. The light coming toward them was getting bigger and brighter, and they could hear the distant rumble of the cars now. Sherri could even swear that the track was vibrating a little.

"Sherri, you've got a daughter to think of. You don't need to be risking your life like this. You need to leave me. Go wait for help to arrive," Scott advised, realizing the chance was slim to none that anyone would get there in time. He was resigning himself to the fact that he might likely die this night. He could accept his fate, but Scott could not accept Sherri dying with him.

"Scott, you can't give up. Help me!" Sherri shouted, kicking at a stake. She had gotten them to move a little. She had to believe that she could somehow get them out in time.

* * * *

Hulk watched Scott and his girlfriend from his hiding place with a smile. *Maybe we'll kill two birds with one...uh train*, he mused, struggling not to laugh out loud. It was at that very moment a violent shudder shook his body. "Oh no!" he said aloud, lowering his head and pinching the bridge of his nose.

* * * *

Wally shook his head and stared about him in confusion. He heard shouting and turned his head to look across a railroad bridge. He could see a train approaching and two people on the track – a man and a woman. The man appeared to be trapped on the track in some way, and the woman was struggling to free him. He could not merely stay off to the side and not help. He scrambled up the embankment and began running up the track toward the imperiled couple.

Scott happened to look up, and when he did, he could not believe his eyes. His bald attacker was running right toward them. "Sherri, look out!" he shouted, pointing over her shoulder – the opposite direction of the oncoming train.

Sherri turned her head to see an large man rushing toward her. She pulled her gun. *I don't have time for this*, she realized. Her heart raced; her breath caught in her throat; and the gun shook in her hand.

"I'm Dr. Wallace Cleaver," Wally identified, throwing his hands up where Sherri could see them. "I only want to help you." he told the woman with the gun, wondering why she had a weapon.

"Don't trust him, Sherri," Scott warned.

Do I have any alternative? she quickly pondered. "I could sure use your help," she said, lowering her gun.

The track had begun to shake under their feet, and Sherri could see the train bearing down on them. She had never been as frightened as she was this very moment. The engineer saw them as well. A loud train whistle pained their ears.

Wally rushed up to Scott. Dropping down, he grabbed hold of one of the anchors and tugged with all his might. Sherri and Scott worked together on the other. Scott was also trying to keep one eye on his attacker. He could not understand why this man suddenly seemed to be trying to help him.

Wally had no idea how he had gotten to this bridge. The last thing he could remember was being at the neurologist's office. But right now, all he could think of was helping these two young people escape harm's way.

Wally jerked again with all his might, throwing all his weight into his pull. The anchor gave way and pulled loose. Sherri and Scott had loosened theirs more as well. Wally pushed Sherri's hand aside and took a firm grasp on the other anchor, putting all his strength and weight behind one last effort.

The train thundered onto the bridge. Scott could see its blinding light shining in Sherri and his attacker's pinched, sweating faces. Their squinting eyes were slits. The track quaked so violently that it felt as if the ties would rip loose and tumble into the river. Earsplitting brakes screeched; a piercing whistle and a massive *boom, boom, boom* reverberated off the steel bridge and all through Scott's body. A putrid smell from the train's scorching brakes singed Scott's nostrils and made him want to gag.

"Get off the track!" he screamed, swinging his arms to the side to direct Sherri. But there was no way she could hear Scott nor was she paying any attention. Sherri was diligently helping to pull on the other anchor.

Scott closed his eyes. If he was not instantly killed when the train hit him, he could not bear to watch Sherri die. Scott could feel the cold steel of the train bearing down on them all. He gritted his teeth, said a silent prayer, and braced for their deaths.

It was at this very instant that he felt the anchor give way. Tons of steel met an off-balance body. Tossed into the air by the train, the flailing individual was hurled over the side of the bridge. A second later, there was a splash in the river below.

Two sets of horrified eyes watched from the side of the bridge, just out of reach of the train. At the last second, Scott had managed to grab Sherri and tumble them both to safety. The engine had screeched past them, barely clearing Scott's feet. Several other freighter cars had rumbled along past them for several more minutes. Then the train finally grumbled to a stop.

A multitude of police lights brightly lit the parking lot off to the side. Lieutenant Gregory and Sergeant Reardon rushed down the side of the track toward Scott and Sherri.

"There's a man in the river," Sherri told the two MNPD detectives. "I have no idea why he decided to help Scott at the last minute. He actually saved his life...probably both our lives...but I believe he was Debbie Gray's psychiatrist. And Scott said he is the one that beat him and pinned him to the track," Sherri relayed in a monologue. She had a glazed look in her eyes as if she was suffering from shock.

"We'll drag the river for the body," Geoff told her. "Right now, there's an ambulance waiting for the both of you. You both need to go to the hospital and be checked out," he instructed. His concern seemed genuine.

He stepped in to help Sherri to her feet. She was surprised to find her legs were still shaking. Geoff passed her off to Nelson, and then he reached to offer his hand to Scott. "Can you walk?" he asked. Like an animal that gnaws off part of its leg to get out of a trap, Scott had worked all the meat off of his ankles trying to get free.

"Yeah...I think so," Scott answered, taking Geoff's outstretched hand.

Scott allowed the lieutenant to help pull him to his feet. He also leaned against him, limping and biting his lower lip as they walked away along the side of the stopped train. When they reached the rock ledge leading into the parking lot, two paramedics took charge of Scott. They lifted him off his feet and carried him to the ambulance.

Scott and Sherri were placed into the same ambulance, since neither appeared to have life threatening injuries. The ambulance bay was brightly lit and the floor vibrated from the running engine. The lights on top could also be seen flashing through the front windows.

The paramedics followed correct medical procedures checking each victim's vitals – shining a flashlight in their eyes and taking their blood pressure. When they saw both individuals were stable, the paramedics stepped out of the bay and closed the back doors, preparing to leave.

Scott lay on his cot, relief rushing over him at still being alive. Sherri got up from her cot, came over to him, leaned down, and kissed his uninjured cheek and the side of his lip. When Scott looked up at her, he saw there were tears in her eyes. "Hey…we're okay," he said, reaching to squeeze her hand.

Sherri grimaced, pulling her hand away, and some tears escaped. When she turned her hand over, Scott could see it was blistered, skinned and cut. "You're hurt. I'm sorry," he apologized. Then, staring up at the metallic roof of the ambulance, he added, "I'm sorry for all of it. It was my own stupidity that put me here in the first place. I knew how dangerous Jeanette was. I never should have tried to take her by myself."

"Shh," Sherri quieted him, brushing his sweaty bangs out of his eyes. "You're alive. That's all that matters," she told him with a bittersweet smile, a few tears escaping and running down her cheeks.

She reached to gently hug Scott just as one of the paramedics leaned his head into the back from up front. "We need to get rolling to the hospital. I need for you to take a seat, ma'am. Or lay down on the cot," he told Sherri.

"Sure," she agreed. She released Scott and went back over to her own cot, taking a painful seat. Her tailbone was bruised from her fall on the rocks.

A few moments later, they were on their way to the hospital. And Sherri had to wonder where Jeanette Peterson might be at this very moment. Sherri's gut told her that this monster was making her escape, but there was nothing she could do about it. She lay back on her own cot and gave thanks that she and Scott were still alive. Their safety was what was most important to her at this very moment.

Sherri decided she would worry about Jeanette Peterson's whereabouts later. For now, she had to trust the MNPD to do their job. Sherri hoped, and prayed, they caught Jeanette and got this beast off the streets once and for all.

Chapter 32

Foiled Again

Jeanette looked over at Susanna. She felt a pang of anger as she accepted that her beautiful little girl now looked like a little boy. Jeanette had cut off all of Susanna's long black curls. She had left the child with very short, boyish-looking hair. Jeanette had also bleached Susanna's hair blond. She even had her dressed in gender-neutral clothing. She knew she could not take the chance of someone identifying Susanna from a photo broadcast in the paper or on television.

2:00 a.m., Susanna was sleeping peacefully in her booster seat. The rental truck Jeanette was driving raced along the expressway. She had left Nashville a few hours ago.

As much as she had hated to do it, Jeanette had left Hulk to finish the job with Scott Arnold and his nosy girlfriend, Sergeant Sherri Ball. She wondered if one, or both of them, were dead now. If all had gone according to plan, then, at the very least, Scott Arnold was now ground beef.

Jeanette took a moment to ponder Hulk. In the end, Hulk had put himself out on a limb for her. They were two killers appreciating the evil in one another. Hulk had returned Susanna to Jeanette. He had driven the cargo van away from Jeanette's house, secured another rental truck, and helped Jeanette unpack everything from the van and put it into this new truck.

Then the two had parted. Hulk had gone to the motel where Jeanette had stashed Scott, bound and gagged. He had beaten Scott silly and taken him to the Railroad Bridge in Nashville. Then he had called Jeanette to let her know their plan had been set into motion. Jeanette had called Sherri from her cell phone as she got onto the expressway and headed out of town. It had been nice having a partner.

Jeanette realized that the MNPD would likely think that she killed Scott, as they did all the other Nashville and Hendersonville victims. She did not care. The only thing they could arrest Hulk for was abetting a criminal for kidnapping Susanna. She bet, as Dr. Wallace Cleaver, he could beat that charge. Scott would be dead, so he could not testify against Hulk.

Jeanette had escaped prosecution once more. She smiled as she stepped down on the accelerator, putting more and more miles between her and Nashville. *On to my new life*, she told herself, already trying to plan in her head where she would settle and what new identity she would ascertain.

The End

Continue the journey....

You have just completed **Sissy Marlyn's** second murder mystery. Don't despair! There will be more engrossing novels to lose yourself in from **Sissy Marlyn**.

Still planned for 2007:

Bowling Green

You will want to pick up the next novel in the "B" Women's Fiction series. Discover what happens to Elizabeth Michaels as she struggles to raise a child whose father she hates.

Jury Pool - Justice

Find out if the killer in the Jury Pool Series is finally brought to justice.

Check the **Sissy Marlyn** website:
www.sissy marlyn. com
often for updates on upcoming novels and appearances.

Thank you!
Sissy Marlyn

Printed in the United States
83079LV00002B/568-582/A